Cagliostro

Also available in this series

Cagliostro

Vicente Huidobro

translated from Spanish by
Warre Bradley Wells

Shearsman Books

Second Edition.
Published in the United Kingdom in 2019 by
Shearsman Books Ltd
50 Westons Hill Drive
Emersons Green
BRISTOL
BS16 7DF

Shearsman Books Ltd Registered Office
30–31 St. James Place, Mangotsfield, Bristol BS16 9JB
(this address not for correspondence)

ISBN 978-1-84861-658-5

First published as *Mirror of a Mage* by
Eyre and Spottiswoode, London, in 1931;
first U.S. edition published by Houghton Mifflin Co.,
New York & Boston, 1931.

First publication in Spanish as *Cagliostro*
by Ediciones Zig-Zag, Santiago, Chile, 1934.

Notice
Every effort has been made to trace the representatives of the
translator's estate but we have had no success. We would be pleased
to hear from anyone who controls the literary estate of W. B. Wells.

CONTENTS

*The author with Lya de Putti (holding his hand) and other actresses,
after winning the award from The League for Better Motion Pictures for the
Cagliostro script (1927). See further details in the afterword to this volume.*

PREFACE

Everybody, no doubt, is more or less familiar with the name of Cagliostro. A man so mysterious, alike in himself and in the circumstances of his life, can hardly fail to interest people, especially those who are connoisseurs of things curious.

But who was Cagliostro?

If we look up his name in an encyclopaedic dictionary— *Larousse,* for example—we find this reference: 'Cagliostro—A clever charlatan, doctor and occultist, believed to be an Italian, born at Palermo, and said to have died in the castle of Saint Leo, near Rome (1743-1795). Had a great success at the Court of Louis XVI and in the Parisian society of that time; played a great part in Freemasonry; was involved in various affairs, including the famous affair of the Queen's Necklace; afterwards removed to Rome, where he was condemned to death by the Inquisition, but this sentence was commuted to imprisonment for life.'

Other encyclopaedias say that nothing is known for certain about his origin, or even about his death. Others again add that he passed himself off as a magician and claimed to be able to make gold and to possess marvellous recipes for increasing the size of pearls, diamonds, and other precious stones; and that he also claimed to know the Elixir of Life. According to some accounts, he carried his audacity to the point of declaring that he could divine the winning numbers in any lottery whatsoever.

On one occasion he solemnly declared that he had already lived for three thousand four hundred years, and that he would live as long again. That nothing should be lacking to complete his legend, it was even said that Cagliostro believed himself to be capable of raising the dead.

All the extraordinary powers of this man, according to these authors, were to be attributed to the fact that he was a clever charlatan, a prestidigitator of the first order. The marvels that are told of him were the result, they say, of collective suggestion; for perhaps this man was more learned than anybody else (here we have a small concession) in certain phenomena of hypnotism and magnetism.

In other words this magician-charlatan, this magician-presti-digitator, worked miracles which were due solely to collective suggestion. Therefore they were not true miracles but false miracles, feigned miracles. He made people believe that he manufactured gold, he made them believe that he possessed the Philosopher's Stone, he made them believe that he enlarged precious stones, and all the rest of it.

This is a curious argument which, in seeking to discredit marvellous things, would explain them away by other things no less marvellous. It rejects one extraordinary thing in the name of another that is equally extraordinary. For it is not to be denied that a man who possesses the power of mass suggestion to such a point that he can make people see whatever he wishes them to see is, at least, as extraordinary as a man who manufactures gold, makes pearls grow, or increases the span of life. The one fact is as marvellous as the others.

Those false men of science of the generation of thirty or forty years ago, who refused to accept anything outside the sphere of eating and digestion, who shied at any phenomenon a little out of the way, and who when they had to explain it tangled themselves up in their reasoning and tied themselves up in their speech to the end of talking nonsense which explained nothing—such men would be laughable if they were not lamentable.

I do not mean to imply that I am a miracle-monger, or that I believe in all the prodigies that are told in old wives' tales—far from it. But it does seem to me that there are many phenomena about which we are as yet ignorant; and that, if we cannot explain them in an intelligible way, it is much better not to try and explain them, but to admit frankly that for the time being they are incapable of explanation. This attitude appears to me to be more dignified and less ridiculous than that of offering half-baked explanations.

Why should we assume it to be impossible that the alchemists of earlier times manufactured gold? Why should we regard this as so extraordinary? Are we not surrounded by the extraordinary? Is it not extraordinary to put a record in a gramophone and out of a disc of pulp or celluloid like this reproduce the human voice? And what about wireless telegraphy, and television, and all the phenomena of electricity? Perhaps there is nothing extraordinary about the fact that a little cable is capable of transmitting, from a distant dynamo, the energy necessary to keep hundreds of tramcars running about a city?

It may be asked: if some alchemists succeeded in making gold, why can we not do so today? This is a very poor argument, for everybody knows that an invention may be lost. We do not know today with any certainty how Archimedes burned the enemies' ships from a distance. Among occultists, moreover, formulas did not pass from hand to hand as they pass today among men of science. These formulae were expressed in intentionally obscure symbols, so that only the highly initiated could discover their secrets.

On the other hand, I think that it will readily be admitted that a man might have invented something, have shown it to his friends, and then have died without ever having been able to explain his processes. Nobody can deny that this could happen, or that it may have happened.

Is there any reason why Cagliostro should not have been precisely such a man? Who can assert, and claim authority for the assertion, that Cagliostro did not make gold artificially, or increase the size of diamonds, or divine the winning numbers in lotteries, or cure sick people who had been given up as hopeless by other doctors? Such an assertion amounts to claiming that the knowledge of all men must necessarily be the same.

Was Cagliostro a charlatan? It is possible that all doctors are charlatans. Attend any session of a medical society. What magnificent charlatanry; and what magnificent assurance in this charlatanry! Read the papers presented to medical societies and institutes merely in the last forty years, and then make a reckoning of all the theories discussed, accepted, and today discredited. What brilliant charlatanry; and what full-bodied assurance in that charlatanry!

What was the great claim of Cagliostro? It was that he possessed certain secrets unknown to his contemporaries, and that he could cure infirmities of the body and especially of the spirit, and that he used these powers to acquire a real ascendancy over men and nations. To what end? Some say that he was the visible representative of certain occult sects which pursued objects unknown. Others say that he desired only to establish on earth a regime of greater social justice and liberty of ideas.

The author of this book has not attempted to follow Cagliostro in all the episodes of his life. I say nothing here of his journeys to England, or of his trial in London, in the course of which his accusers themselves admitted that on several occasions he had given them lottery numbers which proved to be winners. I say nothing either of his journey to Russia and his stay at the Court of Catherine, or of the years which he spent in Italy.

I have confined myself to telling, in the minor key of mystery, his life and legend in France. Towards the end of the reign of Louis XVI France and a large part of Europe were invaded by numerous secret societies, whose activity, unknown to the great majority of people, had a vast influence upon the events of the time. How many happenings whose origin is obscure to us perhaps had their birth in underground retreats where a handful of hunted men plotted by the dim light of a candle!

These societies arose out of the miraculous East. The power of the occult fascinated some of the best minds of the West. Attracted by the lure of these forgotten sciences, they devoted themselves wholeheartedly to the study of alchemy, magic, and all the mysteries of the Kabbalah. Among the initiated only a few chosen spirits can have possessed truly superhuman powers. Admission to these societies involved the most absolute secrecy. Woe to him who betrayed it!

Whence did Cagliostro arrive in France? Whither did he go? These are questions which he always himself desired to leave a mystery. The author has chosen to respect that desire.

The eternal questions which different authors have raised about Cagliostro must be settled in a book more scientific than this. Was Cagliostro a person in the service of a nation or a secret society which aspired to change the general political regime in Europe? Was he a man engaged in hidden designs, or was he simply a man inspired? What mysterious hand, and to what end, guided personalities so strange as those of Cagliostro and the Count of Saint Germain? When Cagliostro said that he had lived for thousands of years, and that he would live for many centuries more, was he speaking of a material fact, or was he rather referring to the revolutionary spirit which he seemed to incarnate in his time?

The best answer to these questions, and to all the accusations of which his name has been the object, is to be found in these words of his own:

> I am of no age and of no place. Outside of Time and Space my spiritual being lives its eternal existence. If I plunge myself in my thoughts which go back over the course of ages, if my spirit aspires towards a way of life different from that which you see around you, I succeed in being that which I desire ... Judge my way of life, judge my actions; say whether they be good and whether you have seen others of greater power. Then concern yourselves neither with my nationality, nor with my rank, nor with my religion.

So much for the personality of Cagliostro.

As for the form of this book, I have only to say that this is what may be called a visual novel, with a technique influenced by the cinematograph.

I believe that the public of today, which has acquired the cinema habit, may be interested in a novel in which the author has deliberately chosen words of a visual character and events that are best suited to comprehension through the eyes.

Some years ago there was much discussion in the intellectual world over the question whether the cinematograph could or would have any influence upon the novel. Recently the periodical *L'Ordre* has been conducting an inquiry into this question here in Paris.

The majority of the replies were foolish. Our gentlemen of the pen feel their pride wounded by the thought that the cinematograph could influence literature. They forget that every invention of men influences men, and above all the sensitive man, the artist.

It is obvious that writing is not the same since the invention of the motor car or of electricity as it was before. Everybody, whether he realises it or not, is subject to the influence of all the inventions of his time. These inventions, possibly without his being conscious of the fact, have filtered through the skin of the man of letters. The result is to be seen not only in the images which he employs, but also in a style of writing which is more nervous and more rapid, which employs more short-cuts and is keener-edged.

I do not mean to suggest that all writers in all their works have been influenced by the cinematograph. But it is undeniable that almost all of them in some of their works, and others in all their works have felt this influence in greater or lesser degree.

Character drawing today has to be more synthetic, more compact, than it was before. Action cannot be slow. Events have to move more rapidly. Otherwise the public is bored. There cannot be large voids or long preliminary descriptions as in the novel of earlier times. In this consists the superiority of the American film at its best over the European; and it has been appreciated here by all true artists, who today make their films *à l'américaine.*

The drawing of characters by means of long psychological processes is finished. Four strokes of the brush, and a living being is painted. Four strokes of the brush, and a situation is painted. Four strokes of the brush, and a landscape is painted. And to paint them well by this method is much more difficult than it was by the old.

We live in an age of pills and tablets. Nobody takes a potion of half a litre for a headache. He takes a tablet of aspirin. We have left potions to our grandfathers.

This book was first published fragmentarily in 'advanced' reviews in 1921 and 1922. It has been completely revised for the present publication. It is my answer to the question whether the cinematograph can influence the novel.

Vicente Huidobro,
Paris, *April,* 1931.

TO THE READER

It may be supposed that the reader has not bought this book in a bookshop, but rather has bought a cinema ticket.

So, dear reader, you are not coming out of a bookshop, but rather going into a cinema. You take your seat. The orchestra launches into a piece of music, which gets on your nerves. It's really ridiculous... But it has to be so, because most of the audience likes it. The orchestra finishes. The curtain rises or, rather, the curtains part, and there appears:

CAGLIOSTRO
by
Vicente Huidobro
etc, etc, etc, etc, etc

Then there appear, in large letters on the screen, an explanatory note concerning the plot, in the briefest possible terms:

INTRODUCTION

Towards the end of the reign of Louis XVI, there sprang up throughout France and most of Europe a great number of secret societies,
whose activities, although unknown to the majority of the populace,
had a great impact on the events of the era.

How many events, of whose origin we are unaware, were perhaps
born in dark underground places, where these persecuted individuals
debated by the half-light of a candle!

These societies had their origins in the miraculous East, and the
power of the Occult so concerned the greatest minds of the West
that they surrendered feverishly to the study of Alchemy, of Magic
and of all the mysteries of the Kabbalah, drawn by the beauty of this
forgotten science.

Among the initiates only a very few chosen ones possessed truly
extraordinary powers.

Admission to these organisations involved total and complete
secrecy. Anyone revealing their secrets was in great danger…

I.

PRELUDE IN A TEMPEST

An eighteenth-century tempest broke that autumn evening over Alsace, blushing in her sleep through her turning leaves and the cheeks of her daughters.

Great clouds, black and full as the belly of a seal, swam in the wet winds towards the West, steered by the skilled hands of the constellation of the Charioteer. From time to time the shrewd stab of a lightning-flash poured upon our stricken panorama the chill blood of a wounded cloud.

It was a night propitious for the hammering of counterfeiters and the galloping of the wolves of History. To the right of the reader are the ruin and the busy forge of the tempest; and to the left are wooded hills.

The stately forest was the instrument of the wind. Like an organ or a sea-cave, it lamented as though all the lost children of the world were wailing for their mothers. All this page which I am writing is crossed by a road full of mire, of pools of water, and of Legend.

At the end of it there appeared suddenly a pair of lights, swaying from side to side like a drunkard singing his way over the horizon. A coach mysterious alike in its form and its colour advances towards the reader, closing upon him to the gallop of its horses, whose heavy shoes of iron make all my novel tremble.

Not to be outdone by the Heavens, the coachman lashed his horses with the lightnings of his whip. The coach came on cleaving through the rain as if through cane-fields in the great plains of the Tropics.

The coach arrives before us. It is upon us, only a few feet from our eyes. The rain beats with spiteful intent upon the driver. Reader, fair or plain, you must step aside a pace or two lest you be bespattered by the wheels of this mystery that passes.

Suddenly the tempest waxed—the lightning blinds our rain-filled eyes—and a flash escaping from its invisible anvil struck one of the horses of that dark coach, which seemed more hearse-like than ever as the horse lay dead upon the road, with its two comrades rearing on their hind legs in righteous indignation. Magnificent was the posture of the coachman as he sought to control his startled steeds—like a monarch in Chariot of State at the edge of the abyss of Revolution.

But, if the coachman alone was impotent to stay the flight of the two horses spurred by terror the dead weight of the dead horse was there to lend him aid. The dead weight of Death acted as a brake upon that excess of Life overflowing through nerves electrified into panic.

The strange door of the strange coach creaked as it slowly opened, and a man, wrapped in a cloak which left nothing visible of him but his eyes, protruded his head from the night within the coach into the night outside to ask what happened.

Do you see his eyes—those eyes phosphorescent as the streams that run over mines of mercury? Those eyes suddenly enriched the night. They are the only light that shines in the obscurity of his life. Look at them well; for those eyes that crossed all the eighteenth century like a live rail are the centre of my story.

One glance of those potent eyes would have sufficed to check a thousand runaway horses. His masterful voice demanded to know how serious was the accident.

Humbly the coachman answered. His timid words seemed to lick the hand of the night.

The tempest waned, as though that one carbonized horse had satisfied its hunger.

The man in the cloak, the man with the extraordinary eyes, descended from the coach to find out where they were. Once he had identified the spot, he set off resolutely along a little path that led towards the hills—a path in the depths of the memory of the years, like a thread across the universe!

As he entered the wood the mysterious person whom our eyes are following inhaled with delight the vaulted fragrance of the trees. He flung back his head to measure their height.

It was a fine wood for the mysteries and the incantations of the arcane words that slept in the Kabbalah.

The wood grew more mysterious at the passage of this man who penetrated it with firm tread. He impregnated it with the warmth of his vitality, so that when he emerged upon the other side of it the wood shrank into something mean and without interest, and the trees shivered with a sense of chill. Leaving the shrunken wood behind him, the man who for a space had breathed life into it, and made it shudder to the marrow of its bones, strode away from it into the background of the landscape.

In the background of the landscape was a building in ruins, an old, abandoned winepress—three walls without a roof, three walls gnawed by the pick of the years of pressing, and, in their midst, a rude courtyard cluttered with stones and beams and days moss-grown.

Entering the old courtyard, the man with the phosphorescent eyes began to stamp upon the ground here and there with his foot. A hollow sound arrested him. He bent down and, smiling to himself, groped for a moment with his hand. He found what he sought, and raised a trapdoor too heavy for a normal man.

A little staircase appeared before him. He climbed down it, and the trapdoor closed behind him like the door of a vault. The mysterious person whom we are following found himself in an underground passage, with its stonework green and mildewed with memories without a name.

At the end of the passage our personage discerned a door. He strode towards it, opened it, and saw before him another narrow passage. Resolutely he advanced along it until he came to yet another door. Here he stopped a moment, in the attitude of a man who listens.

Then suddenly, in obedience to the command in his eyes, without his touching it, the door opened. Before his eyes appeared a great room, in the film style of the Middle Ages. In the middle was a large, rough table of stout wood. On the table lay maps, and round the table were seated a dozen persons, bending forward over the different countries of Europe.

At the sound of the door opening of itself the twelve companions hid their faces in the cowls of their cloaks. The man at the end of the table, nearest to the door, drew his sword and advanced menacingly towards the unknown, who stood silent and unmoved upon the threshold, unmoved and silent, wrapped in his mantle to the eyes.

There was a moment of suspense. Then the cape slid slowly from his shoulders.

The ghostly figure with the drawn sword advanced. The unknown fixed his eyes upon his heart and stayed him in his advance. The threatening sword sank slowly to the ground. Then unknown bent his eyes upon him who presided at the table, and upon whose breast, sewn upon his black tunic, was a cross with a rose in the centre.

'Who are you?' the president demanded, without throwing back his cowl. 'Do you not know the danger you run here?'

The unknown advanced two paces.

'*Ego sum qui sum*,' he answered. 'Danger is for the weak. Am I not in the midst of those of the Rosy Cross?'

The Grand Rosy Cross made a gesture of displeasure at his words, and the other cowled figures gathered around him as though ready to take action against the intruder.

'Your life is in our hands.'

'No,' replied the unknown; 'it is in the hands of him who is hidden behind that wall, the Count of Saint Germain.'

All eyes turned towards the wall at the other end of the room. The wall split down the middle and the two sides rolled back slowly. There appeared the Count of Saint Germain, white-bearded, clad in a long tunic white as his beard, seated on a throne set upon a kind of altar, ringed with lighted candles. With a majestic gesture the old man imposed silence.

The unknown intruder advanced towards the altar, and went down upon one knee. The Count of Saint Germain spoke, and his voice was the voice of a demigod:

'In the name of the brethren of the West I greet Cagliostro, the envoy of the East.'

So spoke the Count of Saint Germain. Then he drew from his finger a beautiful ring, older than the rings of Saturn. He placed it upon the hand of the man of mystery, and addressed him in solemn accents that seemed to echo down from some forgotten century:

'Count Cagliostro, I have willed to you my command that you should come here, because I grow too old; and, knowing your knowledge and your power, I have chosen you to carry on my mission. I conveyed my command to you while you slept, and I have shown you in dreams the way that should lead you to me.'

Cagliostro bowed and made answer:

'I thank you, Grand Master. The ring which you give me is the ray and the key.'

'Tell me, Count Cagliostro, what is the name of your master?'

'The name of my Master is　　　A.'

'The name of your master is　　　L.'

'The name of my Master is　　　T.'

'The name of your Master is　　　H.'

'The name of my Master is　　　O.'

'The name of your Master is　　　T.'

'The name of my master is　　　A.'

'The name of your Master is　　　S.'

'My Master was the wisest of the wise.'

'A master unequalled was your Master.' 'His knowledge went back to Hermes, Enoch, and Elias.'

'Give me your device.'

'L. F.'

'Liberty, Fraternity. How will you propagate it among men?'

'With the eagle and the ewe lamb.'

The Count of Saint Germain produced a little metal box, fashioned in the form of a scroll. He opened it, took out a parchment, and handed it to Cagliostro.

'Here you will find written down that which you need to know, together with the names of those who best may serve you. Never forget that the loss of this document would mean death to many of your brethren.'

'Never will I forget,' Cagliostro answered.

Carefully rolling up the parchment, he placed it in his breast. Face to face a moment stood the two great Mages of one half of the world. Then they embraced one another, exchanging the secret sign of their order—a sign which I may not reveal under pain of death.

Cagliostro approached the others, and with every one of them he exchanged the same sign of salutation. Then he strode towards the door. As he turned once more upon the threshold, the voice of Saint Germain pursued him with a last adjuration:

'I hope, Cagliostro, that our brethren will never have cause to regret this choice.'

From the threshold of the doorway Cagliostro bowed and disappeared.

Hardly had he vanished before the brethren of the Rosy Cross uncovered their faces and hastened to the altar.

'Tell us, Master,' they inquired of the old man, 'who is this man whose eyes shine with the light of stars that shine no more? Where was he made initiate?'

'He is a man, you must know, who comes from the depths of History. He learned the Secret in a century so distant that, in its course through Space that century has already passed beyond the orbit of Jupiter.'

Saint Germain turned to him among the brethren of the Rosy Cross who bore upon his tunic the cross with a rose in its centre.

'Now,' he said, 'you know what it is that you have to do.'

The second leader of the brethren, tall and thin as the shadows that stretch towards the Infinite, bowed his head in assent.

He knew already that which he had to do. What duty was this that lay upon the second leader of the brethren of the Rosy Cross?

Outside, reclining wearily upon the landscape, the old wine-press in ruins, indifferent to all that passed within its breast, seemed to give ear to the silent communion of the stars.

The storm had passed, and the moon waited patiently as an iceberg for the sun to melt her into the familiar oceans of the sky.

Suddenly the trapdoor of the wine-press opened once again, and Cagliostro emerged from the vaults into the landscape.

A few clouds with udders all but emptied strayed towards their distant sheepfold, while others still grazed upon the uplands of the sky, jostling together like handkerchiefs waving farewell, still glistening with the last tears.

An owl, high up upon a bough, bent its heedful head above the night. By the same path that had led him to the wine-press Cagliostro strode back towards his coach and his destiny.

On the King's highway the coach anxiously awaited the hour of his return. The head of the drowsy coachman nodded from the night on one side to the night on the other as he awaited the arrival of his master; and the dead horse, cur loose from the traces of Destiny, awaited the laws of decay.

Cagliostro appeared on the path striding towards his coach. It seemed, as he approached, that he was grown to a stature incredible. He reached the coach, he mounted within it, and the coach set off at a gallop. It was far distant along the highway, and nothing was to be seen of it but its little rear light, shaped as an almond, like an eye that smiled between earth and sky. Then a cloud, fulfilling its mission, trailed along the ground to hide it from the curious eyes of men.

So it was that Cagliostro appeared in Europe. He emerged out of a black coach that came out of mystery into France in the depths of night.

Whence did he come? I have said it already: he came out of the Infinite in a coach escorted by the lightnings, contrary to that prophet Elias who went up into Heaven in a chariot of flames. He came out of the uttermost recesses of legend, out of the deeps of some design of power, traversing all the centuries to the trotting of his steeds, and shaking Time with the creaking of his coach along forgotten ways.

He appeared suddenly in History between two thunder-claps.

II.

EXCELSIOR

For some months past there had been living in the city of Strasbourg a mysterious sage, who had won fame by his marvellous cures.

The whole city talked of him and nothing else, and the tale of his miracles filled the eyes of its citizens with the shining of precious stones.

His house was a house like any other house.

It was situated in a street that was the same as any other street. But inside it was the dwelling-place of a mage, a necromancer with the laboratory of an alchemist, a waiting-room, and a great chamber within which none might set foot. So the house had become a house different from all the other houses, and the street had become a street different from all the other streets—the street of the doctor who cured.

A halo of miracle encircled the house, spread over the whole street, extended throughout the country and then throughout the whole of Europe, reaching out to the four cardinal points of the compass.

The gaze of all eyes, the conversation of all tongues, converged upon the house. Curiosity, admiration, the enthusiasm of the populace caressed its walls; and even the tired moon stopped to stare at it.

Its waiting-room was ever thronged with people. Upon its walls hung more *ex-votos* than in the chapels of the ports that face the seas of constant shipwreck, or of those places famed for their pilgrimages.

*   *   *   *

It was a day of the middle season. In the waiting-room the sick awaited their turn, with their eyes gleaming with good omen—eyes opened wide in the presence of the impossible that had not been seen in the world since the time of the Messiah.

In the next room, laboratory and consulting-room alike, sat Cagliostro at his table, consulting old manuscripts and rare folios, surrounded by packets of herbs, boxes and vials of drugs, and alembics innumerable: all the equipment of the true mage and alchemist.

Three sharp knocks sounded upon the door, and on the threshold appeared the faithful servant of the mage, a young Egyptian by name

Albios, clad after the fashion of his country. Servitor and assistant of his master at one and the same time, Albios had all the fineness of his race, and with it a certain inborn wisdom, an *a priori* knowledge engraved upon his spirit as upon the stones of his native Pyramids.

At the sound of his entrance Cagliostro, like a sleep-walker who returns from a far-off dream, raised his head, immersed in his alchemy.

'The sick are waiting,' Albios announced.

With a curt gesture the mage gave him to understand that he might let them enter. As Albios withdrew, his master gave the last touches to his distillations.

Again three sharp knocks were heard upon the door, and Albios reappeared, ushering in a sick man who lay upon a stretcher, borne by two men. The mother of the ailing youth, with her face irradiated by a last hope, sank upon her knees before Cagliostro. The two bearers withdrew. Her maternal eyes supplicated the Infinite. The Infinite was Cagliostro, and he drew near to visit the sick. Kabbalistic signs were sketched in the air, and fell like astral rings upon the body of the patient; He lay with his eyes closed in sleep.

Taking up a vial, Cagliostro poured its contents into the mouth of the sick man. Then he passed his hand over the sleeping eyes. Returning from their wanderings in who knows what stellar spaces, they opened and fixed themselves anxiously upon the mage. Cagliostro smiled, a smile like a magician's wand, and as he smiled he summoned:

'You are healed. Arise!'

The mother bent over her son as he began to writhe like a man in the throes of death, like a being who, in the very gateway of the Beyond, feels himself seized by some strange power that draws him back again to Earth. The anguished eyes of the sick youth flickered from the mage to his mother, and from his mother to the mage.

Among the skeins of those intertwining glances, Miracle trembled like a great spider.

(*Arraignée du soir, espoir...*)

'Arise and walk! Arise and walk, new Lazarus—my Lazarus!'

Ringing was the voice of Cagliostro, and at his summons a swarm of millenary echoes seemed to awaken and return to life from some far-distant place, lost in the depths of history and geography.

The sick youth revived; he sought to rally himself within his frame; his movements grew stronger,

'Arise and walk! I command you to arise.'

Charged with electric force, the air of the room thrilled and sparkled like a diamond. The star of miracle hung above their heads.

'Arise! Arise, I say—arise!'

The sick man raised his head, sat up, and moved his legs. He stood upright upon his feet.

'Come to my arms, come to my heart, my Lazarus!' cried Cagliostro.

'Come to my arms! I love you because you are my creation. Come to my arms!'

He flung them open wide, wider than a horizon of faith without a cloud.

Trembling, the youth now healed took a few paces forward, and fell upon the breast of the mage, who embraced him tenderly. His mother threw herself upon her knees at the feet of the mage, kissing the hem of his garment.

Of these gestures of gratitude, almost idolatrous, though spontaneous and natural enough, Cagliostro made an end. He helped the poor mother to her feet and led her to the door, giving her some pieces of money to speed her on her way; for, as well as miracle, the mage dispensed also charity. Never did he forget those little things which should make him beloved by the people—and not only beloved, but even deified.

Between his mother and Albios, with his face shining with happiness like the sun, the youth walked out to the next room. There the other sick who were awaiting their turn saw to their astonishment that the cripple was walking. They gathered around him in their excitement.

'A miracle! A miracle!' they cried; 'he has healed him—and he was as good as dead! A miracle, a miracle!'

From the excited group Albios detached a talkative blind man, and led him by the hand into Cagliostro's laboratory.

Guided by Albios, the blind man appeared in the threshold of the doorway. Cagliostro made him sit down beside his worktable. The mage took a pot of ointment, which he kneaded in his hands with leaves of herbs. With the mixture he stroked the eyelids of the blind man, raising them from time to time, like the drop-scene of a lifeless theatre wherein no spectacle has left a trace.

Suddenly Cagliostro stopped in the midst of his operation, and raised his head with every mark of anxiety. What was happening? He laid the pot of ointment on the table, and hastened into the room which lay beyond his laboratory—the mysterious chamber into which none might enter.

Within the chamber was Lorenza, the wife of the healer. She was seated in a chair in the middle of the room, reading.

Even before he had opened the door and drawn back the curtains, Lorenza sensed the coming of Cagliostro. With countenance convulsed and eyes full of dread she rose to her feet, and made as though she would hide herself in the most distant corner. There she crouched upon a couch.

The door opened, creaking on its hinges, the curtains parted, and Cagliostro appeared. 'Lorenza, my dear, why do you always flee from me?'

Slowly and sadly he approached her.

Terror grew in the starting eyes of Lorenza as he drew nearer to her, as though every pace of his imprinted itself upon her pupils.

Cagliostro came beside her, looked at her tenderly, and then, as though he drove away a dream, laid his nervous hands upon her brow. She sank back hypnotised.

Over the face of Lorenza swept a change startling in its suddenness. She smiled, and, drawn by his power, she went towards him. She was hardly more than a girl, beautiful with the beauty of Italy. Ah, how beautiful she was, the brunette with her great dark eyes, full of light and grace!

(Reader, think of the most beautiful woman you have ever seen, and then apply her beauty to Lorenza. So you and I may both spare ourselves a long description.)

As though he drew her by the fetters of his eyes, Cagliostro led her to the chair where we first saw her reading, and made her sit down.

'Tell me, dear Lorenza, tell me what is happening? I felt hostile currents that played about me.'

'My dear lord, so great is your power that you have naught to fear. But, if you bid me...'

Cagliostro laid his hands upon her and bade her speak.

'Go to the house of the Count de Sablons, and tell me what is passing there. Obey!'

With her head flung back, almost automatically, like a sleep-walker, Lorenza began to speak.

'I see into the house of the Count de Sablons ... I see into the Count's library. There is a meeting ... Wait ... They are talking about you ... wait, wait! The Count de Sablons, the Marquise Eliane de Montvert, the Prince de Soubis, the Prefect Gondin, Madame Barret, Doctor Ostertag, the Prince Rolland, and Marcival. ... Madame Barret approaches the Count de Sablons and the Prefect ... wait ... I hear her speaking...

' "Pardon me, Count, but in my opinion this man is nothing but a charlatan."

'Doctor Ostertag comes up to them, declaring that he thinks the same. He says that he does not believe in the wisdom of the mages. De Sablons answers ... Wait, wait ... de Sablons is speaking...

' "In any case since he arrived in Strasbourg the whole city talks of nothing else but his prodigies." The Count is pointing to the Prince de Soubis ... "There you have the Prince de Soubis, condemned to death by every doctor who has seen him. Today, thanks to him, he finds himself completely cured."

'The Prince de Soubis confirms what his friend says. He appears satisfied and grateful. In another group the Prince Rolland is talking excitedly with the Marquise de Montvert. I cannot hear what he is saying. She does not seem to be listening to him. Her eyes wander away and she looks with more interest at Marcival, I hear her asking him...

' "What is your opinion, Marcival?"

' "I believe, Marquise, that he is a man who possesses powers unknown to the generality of men".'

Slowly Lorenza told the scenes that she saw and the words that she heard. Cagliostro, all ears, did not miss a syllable.

'Go on, Lorenza. Do not stop, go on!'

'Oh Sir, the Prefect Gondin is in a furious rage. He is standing in the middle of the room, and seems to be defying you. He strides towards the door and back again in his anger. Now he is speaking, I hear him speaking...

' "In my capacity as Lieutenant of Police of this city I tell you that he is a dangerous man, and that, sooner or later, I shall lay my hands upon him".'

Cagliostro clenched his fists in an angry gesture.

'Wait, Lorenza,' he said; 'sleep on in peace. Rest a while.'

He strode rapidly out of the room.

*   *   *   *

In the house of the Count de Sablons his guests were still debating heatedly. Everyone had a somewhat different opinion, but it was clearly to be seen that they fell into two opposed groups: the partisans and the enemies of the mage. Between the two groups stood out the noble, stately figure of Marcival, with his mystic's eyes full of a flowering of light, serene in his bearing, courtly and reserved in his manner. He was a man impenetrable. He had no need to speak. A single gesture of his dominated all the scene, and a single word from his lips ennobled all the atmosphere around him.

The Marquise de Montvert looked at him with eyes of love. She had no eyes but for him, and she paid no heed to the passionate words addressed to her by the Prince Rolland—the poor Prince who day by day was more enamoured of her, and to whose pleadings she was day by day more deaf.

In vain de Sablons tried to make the voice of common sense heard. In vain he went in agitation from one group to the other. He was a little man, some fifty years of age, with keen eyes that looked at you frankly.

Brusquely, in the midst of the hubbub, the Prefect Grondin rose to his feet. He thumped the table with his fist, and he cried with an air of defiance: 'I should like to see this Cagliostro of yours at close quarters.'

The words had hardly left his lips when the door at the end of the room opened, and Cagliostro appeared upon the threshold, mysterious and smiling, contemplating the effect produced by his apparition.

'You called me—you, Sir ... If I am not mistaken.'

Astonishment and something like dismay were depicted in all faces as Cagliostro spoke. Only Marcival, cold and serene, made a contrast with the other persons who looked at the mage and at one another.

Cagliostro turned towards Gondin.

'Rather than waste your time in attacking me, Sir Lieutenant of Police, you would be better employed in hastening to your own house, where at this very moment someone is trying to break in, to the end that he may seize certain documents of importance.'

Gondin regarded him with a disquiet verging upon terror. He strode towards the door. As he brushed past his new rival he flung a sentence at him.

'I make all speed, Count Cagliostro—even though it be only to put your gifts of divination to the test.'

Hastily the Lieutenant of Police disappeared, slamming the door behind him.

In his turn Cagliostro started to take his leave and withdraw. But the Count de Sablons and his friends pressed around him, begging him to stay a few moments with them. Cagliostro accepted the invitation, and shook hands with those of them he knew—the Prince de Soubis, Madame Barret, and Doctor Ostertag.

Doing the honours of his house, the Count de Sablons led him to the Marquise de Montvert and the Prince Rolland, who never left her side.

'Count Cagliostro,' he said, 'I present you to the Marquise Eliane de Montvert, the most beautiful of the ladies of the Court of France.'

He turned to the Prince Rolland. 'And to the Prince Rolland, who only awaits a proof of your powers to count himself among the most faithful of your disciples.'

Insistent in their curiosity, the Prince and the Marquise begged Cagliostro to give them a proof of his wisdom. Feigning modesty, Cagliostro excused himself.

'We should like to believe in you,' said Eliane; 'we have heard so much talk about your extraordinary powers and your miracles.'

'Ah, yes, Count Cagliostro,' added the Prince Rolland, 'we are eager to believe in you. Will you not deign to give us a demonstration of your gifts?'

Calm and impenetrable, Marcival, leaning against the old marble chimney-piece, surveyed the scene. He seemed to attach no great importance to the curiosity of his friends.

The Count de Sablons conducted Cagliostro to him.

'I present you to the Prince Marcival, a man of enigmas, who knows all tongues and is deeply learned in solar science and philosophy.'

Cagliostro and Marcival shook hands. Then Marcival resumed the attitude he had adopted before the introduction, while Cagliostro and the Count returned to the group around the Marquise.

In a corner, with their noses close together, Madame Barret and Doctor Ostertag were talking in low voices. The doctor murmured into his companion's ear.

'I am going to play a trick upon him, in order to unmask him before his admirers. Will you arrange to have one of my servants come here?'

Madame Barret nodded her agreement, smiled, and went out of the library.

The Marquise de Montvert was still importuning Cagliostro to give a demonstration of his powers in her presence.

'Since your powers are so great, Count, let me see some member of my family who is dead or far from here. For you this should not be difficult; but for me it would be something unique in my life, something so great and a proof so irrefutable that I should suffer none to cast doubts upon your powers.'

Cagliostro bowed his head in assent. He asked the master of the house to be good enough to darken the room. The latter stood up and snuffed out the candles, leaving the chamber in a semi-obscurity relieved only by rare gleams of dim light, a foliage of reflections cast upon the table where stood the sole candle left alight, and on the chair in which, at Cagliostro's instructions, Eliane was to sit.

An *habitué* of such practices, the Count de Sablons went to the mantelpiece, took from it a large fishbowl full of water, and placed it on the table in front of the Marquise, whose eyes, with curiosity, followed his every movement.

At this moment Madame Barret returned to the room. Together with Rolland, Soubis, and de Sablons, she approached the table set for the experiment.

From his own position Marcival watched the proceedings with an air of aloof indifference. Madame Barret murmured a few words into Doctor Ostertag's ear. The doctor rubbed his hands and smiled sardonically.

Standing behind Eliane, Cagliostro placed his right hand at a certain level between the fishbowl and the head of the Marquise. The doubt in the face of the Marquise vanished and gave place to interest in proportion as Cagliostro's hand approached nearer and nearer to the bowl. In it appeared the figures of two men fighting a duel with swords.

The two duellists were fighting in the corner of a garden, at the foot of a staircase. Both seemed to belong to the nobility, and both gave testimony to their skill as swordsmen and familiarity with the use of arms. The vigour of the fight, with its repeated assaults and parries, was not relaxed for a moment, until finally one of the two fell to the ground, wounded in the head.

At this moment it seemed that the stricken countenance of Eliane de Montvert filled the whole room. Inside the bowl the wounded head grew and waxed enormous, more and more enormous until it overflowed the bowl and dominated all the foreground. That head, nothing but that head, with a gaping wound in its brow, gushing blood, stands like a wall before our eyes.

Eliane uttered a cry of horror. 'My husband, my husband!'

She swooned away. The company hastened to aid her and to light the candles.

Marcival made his way to Cagliostro, and there was a ring of severity in his words.

I beg you, Count Cagliostro, to have done with these dangerous experiments.'

Cagliostro fixed his eyes for a moment in surprise upon the man who had dared to speak to him in such a tone. Then he turned aside to busy himself with the Marquise, whom her friends had laid upon a couch. The mage restored her to consciousness and sought to calm her, holding her hands in one of his own and making passes in the air with the other. But Eliane shuddered and sobbed like one possessed. Her eyes were glued to Cagliostro.

'Are you an angel or a devil? … My poor husband was killed in a duel four years ago.' Marcival had taken his place beside the Marquise. He besought her not to speak and lie quiet a moment.

At the door at the end of the room appeared a servant. At the sight of him Madame Barret made a sign to Ostertag, and the two of them hurried to the door, where they exchanged a few words in a low voice. Then they came back in silence, with a smile of triumph on their lips.

*   *   *   *

At the other side of the door, in the spacious corridor, a man was waiting. He was a servant of Doctor Ostertag. The servant of the Count de Sablons appeared at the door leading out of the library, came up to the other, and gave him the orders he had received. As he heard them the first servant assumed a mien of suffering, and, taking his companion's arm, went towards the library.

Once inside it, the two servants approached Doctor Ostertag. The one who appeared to be suffering made a hasty signal to his master, indicating that he understood his role. Ostertag went up to

Cagliostro, who was talking animatedly among the group around the Marquise, now recovered from her indisposition.

'My dear mage,' said the doctor, 'I would like to consult you about a sick man whose case is really extraordinary.'

Cagliostro readily agreed, and turning towards the sick man looked at his eyes, felt his pulse, and after completing his hasty examination smilingly shook his head in a vaguely affirmative gesture. The guests gathered curiously around.

'What is the matter with this man, Count Cagliostro?' asked Madame Barret.

Cagliostro looked at the man again, and turned him round two or three times on his heels. Then he shook him roughly and gazed into space.

'Too much bile in the stomach of Doctor Ostertag,' he answered.

As he spoke he bowed by way of farewell, and walked rapidly out of the room, closing the door behind him.

Doctor Ostertag bit his lips, and his friend Madame Barret looked disconsolate over the triumph of the mage. The others mocked at their suspicions and the doctor's discomfiture.

* * * *

Meanwhile, in Cagliostro's laboratory, the blind man was awaiting the return of the mage with what patience he could muster. Beside him was Albios, seeking to keep him amused by recounting a thousand adventures and achievements of his master.

Cagliostro appeared on the threshold of the inner door. He flung his hat and cloak on a chair, took up the pot of ointment from the table, and resumed the interrupted operation.

'Forgive me, my friend, but an accident compelled me to leave you for a few moments,' he said, in the friendly voice which he ever affected when he addressed the humble.

* * * *

Outside, in the streets of the city, the bats were fluttering back and forth through the air, seeking to attract the night.

Obediently, heavy as a great, black cloud, the night fell over all Alsace, and perhaps over all the world.

Not far away, in another quarter of the city, the visions of the seer also were fulfilled.

In the office of Gondin, Prefect of Police, a light flickered in the darkness, and the ghost who flitted through it, with shrouded head, ransacked the drawers of the prefect's desk and writing table, caring nothing for the disorder that he left behind him.

At the very moment when the phantom seized a document and thrust it into his pocket, the office door opened, and the prefect appeared with one of his men, holding a lighted candle aloft.

As he saw the door open the thief leapt out of the window. The prefect flung himself upon his tracks, but in his haste he stumbled over a chair and fell to the ground. Quickly the servitor helped him to his feet, and he ran to the window. It was too late. The thief had disappeared.

In a fever of anxiety Gondin collected the papers scattered about the floor. Desperately he sought everywhere for the document that most concerned him. It had vanished with the thief who had robbed him of it. Seizing his hat as though he wreaked his vengeance upon it, the prefect dashed from the room. Behind him his servant leant again out of the window, peering in all directions. There was a hint of mockery in the obscurity of the night that spread impenetrable before his eyes.

In his laboratory Cagliostro was finishing his operation on the blind man. He fastened a bandage over his eyes, and handed him the balsam which should work the miracle. But neither was he neglectful of the balsam of his own words.

'Three days more, and you will be healed.' With Abios leading the way, he accompanied the patient to the waiting-room. There he saw how many people still were waiting. He closed the door.

'Nobody else today,' he told his servant.

Cagliostro went back to his work-table. The old hooks and rare manuscripts heaped upon it were his life's passion. Immersed in them he could let whole years go by. You had only to look at him to understand what fascination he found in the extraordinary secrets that he wrenched from their obscure symbols.

He read and experimented, studied and applied his findings, verified his tests. He took a vial and poured into it a few drops of the contents of another. Then he added a small measure of a dark powder. Curiously he contemplated the result against the lamp-light.

He raised his head, and the shadow of a smile was sketched upon his lips. With the utmost care he laid the vials back upon the table, and then he stole on tip-toe towards the door of the waiting-room. He grasped the handle of the door, waited listening for a moment, and suddenly pulled the door open, hiding himself behind it. Propelled forwards by his own impetus, the Prefect Gondin found himself jerked halfway across the room.

Cagliostro stood looking at him with a diabolical smile.

'Whither away so hastily, Sir Lieutenant?'

The prefect swung around sharply, with his eyes starting out of his head. His face was a picture of anxiety. Then pleading showed itself in his eyes.

'You were right ... I have been robbed of a document of the utmost importance. I beseech you to aid me to recover it.'

Like a sentence delivered by a judge fell Cagliostro's terse answer. 'I will do nothing for you, Monsieur Gondin. That shall be all my vengeance.'

The two men stared each other in the eyes. All the sparks of hatred leapt into the air as the edges of their glances rasped together.

* * * *

More infuriated than ever against Cagliostro was Gondin, Prefect of Police, and he could not reconcile himself to his rebuff. The next day, after the happenings which we have just related, he received Doctor Ostertag and Madame Barret in his office. Cagliostro's enemy trio were resolved to fashion a plan that should bring him to ruin.

Making no effort to disguise his wrath, Gondin paced back and forth through the room as he told his friends what had happened the

night before. Madame Barret and the doctor urged him to act with
the utmost energy. It was necessary to deal a decisive blow, and make
an end of this wizard once and for all. For a wizard he undoubtedly
was, declared the good lady—whether her spitefulness was due to
some cause which she might not have been ready to confess or simply
to the fact that the mage had refused to aid her in some private
enterprise. Her passion for intrigue was notorious throughout the
city.

Yes, one must be done with hesitations once and for all, reflected
Gondin. Rapidly he decided to translate his thoughts into action. He
marched upon his writing-table, seized a piece of paper, and started
to write. From time to time he looked up from his writing towards
his friends.

'I'll show you, I'll show you!...'

In Lorenza's chamber, Cagliostro stood beside her and reproached
her gently for her coldness towards him.

'You have no love for me, Lorenza, save only when you are under
the spell of my powers. In spite of all my passion for you, you do not
love me.'

Sometimes she looked at him in terror, sometimes she looked
at him in compassion; but it was plain to see that, if she could, she
would flee far away from the sight of him.

'If I would let you follow the urgings of your heart, you would
flee far from me ... and yet you know well that I love you, that you
are all my happiness, the only thing in this world that I adore. And
you know, too, that I have need of you—that, without you, I could
not realise my plans, my great designs.'

'Your mean your ambitions—your thirst for domination.'

'No, Lorenza; my plans for humanity. It may be that there is still
in my spirit the lust of ambition; but do not forget that no lever is to
be disdained. And remember, too, that elsewhere you were treated as
a Queen; nor did the homage and the tribute of all offend you—nay,
quite the contrary.'

'Yes, but then I did not fear you as I fear you now. Now I believe
that you have made a pact with the Evil One. So many strange things
have I seen you do. Oh, my God, my God, I would not be damned

because of you! Once, indeed, I loved you, my heart was all yours; but tell me, when have you ever thought of my heart? But there was a time when I loved you…'

'And now you love me no longer? Have you no tenderness left for me?'

'No, I have none left. Today I hold you to be the Devil himself; and I feel that a day will come when I shall hate you.'

'Silence, woman, silence! I the Devil?'

'So strange are the things you do that the idea haunts my soul beyond all exorcising.'

'Lorenza, I would have your love. Look at me. Can you not see that in your presence my eyes are ever on their knees?'

'Oh, your eyes—your dreadful eyes; your eyes wherein there lurks a claw!'

'Love me as I love you, and I will make you Queen of the World.'

Timidly Lorenza's eyes looked up at him and down again, looked up once more and were veiled, but unafraid.

'And what shall it profit me to be Queen of the World if I lose my own soul? I swear to you that only by the force of your diabolical powers am I tied to you. In the depths of my soul I begin to hate you.'

Cagliostro loved her, and her words were like the thrust of a dagger in his heart. The wound bled beyond all stanching, and the anguish of it was mirrored in the face of the mage.

There is no mastering of love; and the conflict between love and ambition is implacable.

'You talk like a schoolgirl. What means this nonsense about losing your soul? What folly is this that would make me the Devil?'

'I do not know. I do not know. What avails it to dispute matters whereon we may not understand each other? I do not love you. Let that suffice. I have lost the faith I had in you.'

'You do not love me? So be it. But I still have need of you.'

Bending over Lorenza, Cagliostro took her head between his hands, and switched upon her the electric current of his eyes. And as she sank inanimate beneath his power, there spoke the voice of Cagliostro.

'Since I may not make you love me by my tenderness, then shall you love me by virtue of my power.'

He kissed her upon the brow. Submissive to the potency of his magic, Lorenza looked up at him as he stood beside her, and all at once she was all affection, and in her mien there was all sweetness and all warmth. Cagliostro caressed her and kissed her hands. But it was plain to see that he rode his passion with a sharp curb, lest it should bolt too far. Perhaps it was because of the unworthiness of taking a love unshared; perhaps it was because he knew that, with her virginity, this woman would lose those qualities that made of her a precious instrument of his will.

For love is perilous. Love makes one forgetful of all things else— even those things that matter most in the lives of men.

Cagliostro looked at Lorenza as she lay there, freely offered to him, become a plaything between his hands, shorn of her will, all defenceless. His voice was tender as he bent over her again.

'Lorenza, my love, tell me what is passing at this moment in the house of Gondin.'

'Do you command me?' asked Lorenza, pallid and as if asleep.

'Yes, I command you. Go thither and tell me what you see.'

Lorenza spoke as if from another world. 'They are tying a letter to the wing of a pigeon … The Lieutenant of Police, Madame Barret, Doctor Ostertag…'

Cagliostro bent closer to listen to Lorenza's tale.

*   *   *   *

At a window of his office, the Prefect Gondin, with those inseparable enemies of Cagliostro, Doctor Ostertag and Madame Barret, beside him, tied the letter which he had just written to the wing of a pigeon. The innocent pigeon was fated to carry a message—perhaps a sentence, perhaps a condemnation.

Delicately Gondin held the pigeon, and on the sill of the window he let it go free. The pigeon sped away like an arrow—or, rather, it would have sped like an arrow, were it not that this simile has been overdone.

Complacently the trio watched it vanish in the distance.

In the mysterious chamber of Lorenza the wife of the mage, sitting stiffly in her great armchair, with head thrown back and hypnotised eyes fixed upon the ceiling, went on with her tale-telling. Cagliostro stood beside her, smiling.

As if jerked by a spring Lorenza rose to her feet, seized Cagliostro by the arm, and drew him to the window. She opened it. She looked up into the sky. She had seen something. Cagliostro followed her eyes and saw it too.

'The carrier pigeon, with the message tied to its wing, was following its path through the sky from cloud to cloud.

On one balcony stood the trio of Doctor Ostertag, following with anxious eyes the flight of their discreet emissary.

On a second balcony Cagliostro, with his lips wreathed in a smile of triumph, made magnetic passes in the air towards the line of the pigeon's flight.

It was a duel between the two balconies. Here our two open windows assume a life of their own, a life like that of men, a life of tragedy, full of expectation and of anguish.

* * * *

The pigeon in the sky was the focal point of all the world's gaze. But amid all that staring was a glare of bale, a glare predominant, a glare that mastered all others in its fierceness: the glare of Cagliostro.

Distractedly the pigeon started to fly in circles, to revolve in an orbit around an eye unseen. It strayed from its course. Cagliostro raised his hands towards it, and pulled them sharply back towards him as though he held the string of a kite between his fingers.

Seized with a strange vertigo, such as it had never known before, the pigeon lost all sense of direction. As though it had been struck by a shot, it tumbled out of the sky down the rope ladder cast up by Cagliostro's eyes. It fell upon the window of Lorenza's chamber.

Cagliostro took it gently in his hands.

The second balcony had triumphed over the first.

With the pigeon in his hands, Cagliostro led Lorenza back to her chair, untied the letter, looked at it back and front, and held it up to the light. Then he placed it against Lorenza's forehead.

Read me this message,' he bade her. Lorenza's head is a close-up before our eyes, swollen gigantically by our common curiosity. Her brow dissolves, and in the place of it appears the letter, so that its text is plainly to be read:

> 'To Monsieur de Sartines,
>   Prefect of Police, Paris,
>
>   In accordance with your wishes I have taken steps to prevent the Marquise de Montvert from arriving in time for the fête which is to be given by the King. Your *protégée* will thus be able to take her place. As for Count Cagliostro, I am informed that he also intends to set out for Paris. I agree with you that he is a dangerous person. I suggest that you have him arrested upon some pretext. I am dispatching further advices to you by courier.
>
>   Greetings,
>   Gondin.'

Thanks to the clairvoyance of Lorenza we have read the letter, and the head and face of the medium resume their normal size. They are reduced in scale five times.

With a quick, angry gesture Cagliostro withdrew the letter from Lorenza's brow. He tied it again to the wing of the pigeon, and took the bird back to the window, where he let it go free once more.

For the second time the pigeon soared into the air and resumed the flight that for a moment had been interrupted. Cagliostro, with a smile of satisfaction on his lips, turned towards Lorenza.

'Tonight we leave for Paris.'

*   *   *   *

Prince Rolland had come to take leave of the Marquise de Montvert on her departure for Paris. He seized the occasion to declare his love for her for the thousandth time.

In the salon of the Marquise's palace, the servants were assembling her baggage for her journey. Through the door at the end of it was to be seen another chamber, smaller and more intimate than the first.

At her escritoire the Marquise sat writing. A servant appeared at the threshold, came up to her, and announced that the Prince had come to call upon her. Eliane made no effort to conceal her gesture of boredom, but told the servant to bid him enter. She went on writing, and she did not stop until the Prince appeared at the door of the salon.

Trembling like a child, Rolland advanced towards the Marquise. He held her hand long as he kissed it. She invited him to be seated. Anxiety was written upon his face as he obeyed.

'Eliane, you know what I have come to tell you once again. You are never out of my mind, I can think of nothing else but you. Because I must, I beg of you to tell me whether I may hope...'

Cutting short the Prince's words, the servant appeared again.

'Monsieur de Marcival,' he announced.

The Prince could not hold back an angry gesture. Radiantly Eliane rose to her feet and hastened to meet Marcival. He saluted them both with equal cordiality. Rolland acknowledged his salutation with a curtness that verged on the ridiculous. The lips of Marcival wore his usual calm smile.

Marking the manner of the Prince, the Marquise went to her table, took up the letter which she had been writing, and handed it to Rolland.

'My dear Prince, since Marcival has interrupted our conversation, you may read the continuation of it here.'

Rolland read the letter, and his mien was that of a man profoundly dejected. He put the letter back in its place on the table, and bowed slowly to Eliane. She smiled. He made a frigid gesture of farewell to Marcival, and left the room.

* * * *

Outside the house of Eliane de Montvert the evening fell with that sadness proper to the fall of evening.

It fell, of course, elsewhere as well, but that is a matter which does not concern us.

The coach of the Marquise was waiting at the door, with the patient coachman asleep on his seat, after the manner of all coachmen who know their business.

A group of men with all the marks of knaves hid themselves behind the trees in the road or around the corners of the neighbouring houses as they saw Prince Rolland coming out of the palace of the Marquise.

The Prince had scarcely disappeared when these ill-favoured men reappeared and flung themselves upon the Marquise's coach. Knocking the coachman off his seat, in the twinkling of an eye they left him rolling on the ground and drove the coach away, lashing the horses.

* * * *

Cagliostro was working in his laboratory when Albios entered to announce a visitor in the person of Prince Rolland.

'Ask him to be good enough to come in.' Rolland appeared, and advanced towards Cagliostro with arms outstretched. The poor Prince appeared to be in desperation. The need of a helper, the conviction of his own impotence, had led his steps to the house of the mage.

He recounted to Cagliostro the scene which we have just seen passing in the palace of the Marquise, and told him of the letter which she had given him to read.

'My beloved Marcival, I know that I can never win your love. You are above all human feelings. You are friendly towards me only because your sensitiveness feels my devotion. Ever immersed in study and meditation, you stand upon the edge of life, while I—poor I— still all too human…'

So far had read the letter of the Marquise when the Prince had laid it down. Those few sentences had been enough to leave him desolate and reveal to him how idle were his attentions.

Pityingly Cagliostro looked upon his visitor. He saw that in his face sadness had taken the place of pride. His love was hopeless, and so he had come to supplicate the mage.

'I love her—I adore her … My only hope is in your aid.'

Moved by Rolland's entreaties, Cagliostro promised to do what he could to help him. Gratefully the Prince, once more inspired with hope, seized his hands and offered himself to him unconditionally, for any service he could render him.

The Prince was halfway to the door when he retraced his steps, with the air of a man who remembers something of importance.

'Secret for secret,' he exclaimed. 'You must know that Doctor Ostertag has assembled the leading doctors of the city at his house, to the end of moving them to denounce you as an impostor.'

Cagliostro could not restrain a wrathful movement, which would be imperceptible if our eyes were not fixed upon him. Then, once more master of himself, he accompanied the Prince to the door with an air of indifference.

Alone again in his laboratory, Cagliostro stood a moment absorbed in his thoughts. His face was grave and stern. Brusquely his eyes hardened. He had taken a decision. Without further hesitation he strode to a cupboard in a corner of the room. He selected three vials, of which one was empty. Into this he poured a part of the contents of the other two. Then he dissolved some tablets, and filled another vial with the solution. Placing the two vials in his pocket, he flung on his cloak and hat and walked quickly out of his house into the street.

*   *   *   *

In the little, more intimate chamber of the Marquise de Montvert, Eliane went into ecstasies in the presence of Marcival. She recalled the first day that they had met. Since that day she had thought of no other man but him. From the first moment she had known that he was a man different from all others, a kind of mystic aloof from all the preoccupations of life, a pure spirit, utterly disdainful of things material and ever reaching out towards the infinite: a true ascetic.

With some solemnity depicted in his looks Marcival listened to her. You could sense in him a protective sympathy for Eliane, but not a human passion.

Laden down with valises and travelling bags, a servant descended the stairway leading to the street. He saw the coachman lying unconscious, stretched upon the ground. He saw that the coach had disappeared. Letting fall his baggage he ran back into the house.

Like a bullet he shot through the outer salon, flung himself into the second, and told his lady that the coach had disappeared and that the coachman had been attacked and lay stretched upon the footpath like a dead man.

Eliane looked at him in dismay. Marcival, who did not seem unduly disturbed, essayed to calm her. But loudly the Marquise cried to her servant.

'Begone, and lose no time! Ransack the city, pay what they ask you … I must have a coach, cost what it may!'

As the servant went out again at a run Marcival strolled to the window and looked out into the street.

'If this has been done deliberately,' he said, 'you will have difficulty in finding a coach at liberty.'

*   *   *   *

In the surgery of Doctor Ostertag the five leading doctors of the town, together with the Count de Sablons, were assembled. All of them, with the exception of the Count, were disputing about Cagliostro.

It was an insult to men of science, Doctor Ostertag asserted, that Cagliostro should be allowed freedom to exercise the profession of medicine. He turned to the Count de Sablons, the only partisan of Cagliostro among those present.

'Your Cagliostro is nothing more than an impostor, who practises medicine without right and with no knowledge of it.'

The other doctors agreed, and expressed approval of what Ostertag had to say. They were not likely to do otherwise, since from the day of Cagliostro's arrival in the city their patients had deserted them for the house of the mage. This was the vengeance of empty waiting-rooms upon the laboratory full of miracles.

At this moment the door opened and Cagliostro appeared, with a frozen smile upon his lips and a diabolical look in his eyes.

The other doctors looked at one another in surprise. Only Doctor Ostertag boldly fixed his eyes upon the intruder, giving Cagliostro back glare for glare.

'I expected you,' he said in a resolute voice. 'I know your ways, and I am not afraid of you.' Slowly Cagliostro walked towards Ostertag until they stood face to face.

'You have thrown doubt upon my knowledge, and, what is worse, you have more than once uttered calumnies about me. I demand immediate satisfaction.'

The doctors exchanged glances of dismay. Anxiously the Count de Sablons asked himself what was about to happen. Ostertag's answer was disdainful.

'I am a man of science, and I am not versed in the usage of arms. But I hold myself at your disposal.'

'There are other means,' said Cagliostro. 'Let us seek one appropriate to your science. So may we have occasion to prove our knowledge one against the other. I propose to you a duel by poison.'

'If that be the case, I accept your challenge.' 'Very good. You will prepare a poison which I shall drink, and I shall defend myself against death with my antidote. You will take my poison, and defend yourself with the best of your antidotes. We shall see who will be able to save himself and who will perish. This should be an interesting duel, worthy of us who call ourselves men of science.'

Gathering around Ostertag, the other doctors sought to dissuade him from the duel. Beside himself, feeling his dignity insulted, he refused to listen to reason. He led his friends to the other end of the room, where was to be seen a cupboard full of drugs and vials and boxes of every shape and size.

First Doctor Ostertag and his colleagues compounded the poison for Cagliostro to take, and then the antidote for the doctor to drink to save himself from Cagliostro's poison. Detaching himself from the group, one of the doctor's friends filled a bottle with water and placed it with two glasses on a table in the middle of the room. Seeing that Cagliostro was talking carelessly with the Count de Sablons, he invited him to make ready his potion and offered him the glasses which he had laid upon the table.

'I am already prepared,' replied Cagliostro.

The Count de Sablons seemed in despair over his failure to prevent the duel.

Doctor Ostertag approached the table, followed by his group of doctors. One of them carried two more glasses—one with the poison and one with the antidote.

In his turn Cagliostro stepped to the other side of the table. Into one of the glasses laid upon it he poured his poison and into the other his antidote.

Face to face, divided only by the width of the table, stood Doctor Ostertag and Cagliostro. The eldest of the doctors, assuming the duty of judge of the duel, ceremoniously exchanged the glasses containing the poisons prepared by the two men who were about to drink to each other's deaths. He placed the poison of Cagliostro in front of Ostertag, and the poison of Ostertag in front of Cagliostro. Beside the poisons stood the antidotes of each.

The judge raised his hand and invited them to drink.

Cagliostro and Ostertag took up the glasses.

At the judge's signal Cagliostro drank his without hesitation, and immediately afterwards swallowed his antidote. Doctor Ostertag had raised his glass to his lips, but he could not bring himself to drink its contents. The glass trembled in his hand, and his hesitation turned into terror as he saw that his poison had taken no effect upon Cagliostro.

Indignantly Cagliostro fixed his eyes upon him. They glared at him implacably.

Before the command in the glance of Cagliostro Doctor Ostertag trembled. He flung back his head, and almost mechanically he drank the poison prepared by the mage.

The eyes of the satisfied Cagliostro softened.

Greedily Doctor Ostertag reached for his glass of antidote and drained it at a gulp. The two men stood face to face for a moment of anxiety in which tragedy sowed a heavy silence.

Cagliostro smiled a little, while the eyes of Doctor Ostertag watched him in a fever of anxiety.

The seconds eyed them breathlessly.

Their eyes grew round with dread as Ostertag began to display the first symptoms of poisoning.

Calm and impenetrable, Cagliostro still smiled to himself. The Count de Sablons looked anxiously from one to the other.

The coursing of the venom through the veins of Doctor Ostertag revealed itself in convulsions ever more violent. His face became distorted. He choked and reeled into a chair, with his eyes bulging out of his head and his hands clenched. The doctor writhed like a beast in agony.

The men of science hastened to lend him their aid.

Without blinking an eye, without betraying the least emotion, Cagliostro surveyed the scene. Then he took up his cloak and his hat, and turned towards the door, an impassive victor. The Count de Sablons ran after him, and detained him as he was crossing the threshold.

The Count entreated him. Would he not succour Ostertag? Cagliostro washed his hands of the matter. The punishment was well deserved. It would serve as a lesson and a warning to all the sceptical.

'Save this man,' de Sablons implored him. 'You must not stain your hands with a crime of vanity.'

After a moment of doubt Cagliostro felt his humanitarian instincts triumph within him. He turned back on his tracks and strode to the couch on which they had laid Doctor Ostertag.

The poor doctor was in the last convulsions of his agony. Vainly his friends fought against death. They confessed themselves powerless to save him.

Contemptuously Cagliostro put them aside. Shamefaced the doctors stood back and left the field free to the mage, whom but a few moments before they had so much disdained.

Cagliostro drew from his pocket his vial of antidote, raised the head of the dying man, forced his lips and his clenched teeth open, and poured down his throat all that was left of the contents of the vial. Then he drew away and waited for a moment.

Slowly the dying agonies of the doctor grew less acute. Cagliostro bent over him, and made above him magnetic passes and mysterious signs which perhaps aided the working of his antidote.

Scarcely able to believe their eyes, the doctors watched his every movement.

Cagliostro laid his hand on the doctor's damp forehead and raised his lids.

'He will live,' he pronounced.

The Count de Sablons wrung his hands by way of showing his gratitude. Smiling at his friend, Cagliostro picked up his hat again and marched arrogantly toward the door.

The doctors bowed before him as he passed. Cagliostro turned upon the threshold. 'Knowledge,' he said, 'is not for all. There are things it is given only to some of us to know.'

He left them gaping.

* * * *

Meanwhile, in her salon, Eliane de Montvert was continuing her conversation, so often interrupted, with that strange man Marcival. A woman in love forgets her troubles, however serious they may be, when she is face to face with the man she loves.

The servant, returning from a vain quest for a coach up and down the town, recalled them again to reality.

'There is no coach to be had for the next two days.'

Eliane turned towards Marcival in despair. 'What am I to do?'

But Marcival was as aloof as ever from the little problems of daily life, and indifferent as ever to all human vanities.

'Why distress yourself so about it? To what end do you pay so much heed to this world's banalities? You should look towards higher things, you should disdain things material.'

For all his words of counsel, the Marquise could not so lightly resign herself to lose her place at Court, and see it taken by another who most assuredly would keep it for ever.

'It is evident that I am the victim of a base intrigue. Someone has an interest in keeping me away from Court.'

She had hardly spoken when the old servant appeared on the threshold in the greatest excitement,

'My lady, my lady, there is a coach below.' Eliane darted to the window, opened it, and leant out, looking down into the street. The brightness of the sky that she let in was reflected in her face.

'There is indeed a coach that waits before my Gates.'

Enraptured in her surprise, the Marquise turned back into the room.

Marcival, seated in his chair, was looking towards the door of the outer salon. He was watching a letter that slid beneath it. As he watched it, as though he guessed something, he smiled sadly.

Intrigued, with her eyes rounded into question marks, Eliane approached Marcival. His finger pointed to the paper under the door. The servant hastened to pick up the letter, and handed it to the Marquise. Her nervous fingers tore it open and she read it aloud.

'My lady, here is a coach. Set out for Paris without losing a moment. Your enemies do not know that I am on your side.'

Surprise and satisfaction warred for mastery over the fair face of Eliane de Montvert. A question burst from her lips.

'Who is my guardian angel that calls up coaches when there is none to be had?'

'Your guardian angel calls himself Cagliostro,' replied Marcival; and there was sadness in his voice.

The astonished Marquise stood for a moment lost in her thoughts. Marcival came up to her to take his leave. Tenderly she looked at him as she gave him her hand and he raised it to his lips. Emotion held them silent for a moment. Then she signed to her servants to be quick, and accompanied Marcival to the door.

* * * *

Our good Prefect of Police, Monsieur Gondin, was sitting at the table in his office. A sound, scarcely perceptible, made him raise his head. His wide-open eyes saw a letter gliding under the door of his office.

In three strides the prefect was at the door.

He wrenched it open, and looked up and down the corridor. There was nobody to be seen. He shut the door again, picked up the letter, opened it and read it.

> 'The Marquise de Montvert, at the moment of leaving Strasbourg, desires me to present you her compliments.
>
> COUNT CAGLISOTRO.'

The prefect was beside himself with rage. The mage had beaten him again. He bit his lips till they swelled, as though he savoured vengeance.

*   *   *   *

The Marquise de Montvert sped towards Paris to arrive in time for the fête at Court.

Raising a great cloud of dust behind it, the coach of the Marquise drove at a gallop along the road for Paris.

Watching from the top of a hill we can follow it with our eyes until it disappears around a bend in the road.

*   *   *   *

The city of Strasbourg was weeping over the departure of its benefactor.

Inconsolable in their grief, an immense multitude had gathered in front of the house of Cagliostro. The people of the town flocked around another coach that stood waiting at a door.

At the sight of Cagliostro, followed by Lorenza and Albios, the crowd swayed and men doffed their hats as though in the grip of a mystical devotion. Many went down upon their knees, while others ran to the mage and kissed the hem of his garment. Women raised their children towards him as though beseeching the great healer to give them his benediction.

Cagliostro stretched out his hand over his worshippers, Then he and his companions climbed into the coach. Slowly, with all the people following it, it made its way through the city.

It reached the gates, and the road lay straight before it.

With all their hearts drawn after it, the populace watched it drive away.

A paling orb of greatness, the setting sun seemed to sink down to earth. The coach of Cagliostro dwindled in the distance. Far away upon the horizon it vanished into the disc of the sun.

III.

ON THE PEAK

It was some months later when Abraham Lemberg, the jeweller, was visited once more by a gentleman unknown to him, who for the fourth time had come to exchange an ingot of gold for currency of the Realm.

Beyond all question Abraham Lemberg was one of the richest jewellers in Paris. This day he was working behind his counter, drawing sketches of precious stones which he was minded to have cut and set.

The door which gave upon the street opened, and Albios appeared, clad in European costume. Lemberg raised his head from his papers, and stepped towards the counter with his face wreathed in smiles.

From under his cloak Albios took an ingot of gold and laid it upon the counter, With unconcealed curiosity the jeweller looked at it, then he picked it up and carried it into the room behind his shop. There he weighed it and tested the metal. But from time to time, as he worked, he looked under frowning brows towards the gentleman unknown.

The verification of the ingot was finished.

From his strongbox the jeweller took two bags full of money. He poured their contents out before Albios. The Egyptian counted the number of pieces. Satisfied with his reckoning, he put the money-bags in his pocket and went out. The probing eyes of Lemberg followed his customer.

On the jeweller's threshold Albios swung himself into the saddle of a magnificent Arab steed and set off at a gallop. He disappeared round the corner of the street.

The jeweller was on his way back to his inner room when Marcival appeared at the door of his shop. Hearing the footsteps of the new-comer, Lemberg turned round and came back again to his counter.

Marcival had something to ask him.

'I am told that you have some gold of matchless purity. Could you sell me a little?'

The jeweller replied that he could. He showed his new customer the ingot which he had just bought, together with some pieces of gold which he had from the same source. He compared these pieces with the ingot to demonstrate their identity.

Marcival selected a small piece, Lemberg weighed it for him, and picked up the money which Marcival counted out upon the counter.

Shrewdly the jeweller looked at his customer. 'This is without a doubt the purest gold that I have ever handled.'

'I quite agree with you,' said Marcival.

He took up his little packet, and was gone.

*   *   *   *

That very same day Abraham Lemberg, the jeweller, hastened to the quarters of Monsieur de Sartines to acquaint the Lieutenant of Police with his suspicions.

Seated at the table in his office, Monsieur de Sartines listened to the jeweller's tale with the utmost attention.

It might be worthwhile, Abraham Lemberg suggested, to know whence this mysterious young man, who every score days presented himself in his shop, obtained so rare a gold. This might be a band of robbers with which they had to deal; or, again, he might be acting on behalf of some notorious pirate. In any case the jeweller had laid his information. He washed his hands of any consequences that might arise.

The Prefect Sartines summoned to his office two men in his confidence, and placed them at the jeweller's orders. Lemberg bade them follow him, telling them as they went what matter was in hand and what it was that they must do.

*   *   *   *

On the top floor of an old house, Marcival had chosen as his lodging a humble garret.

It was a room as strict, severe, and sober as its guest. A bed, a table, a candlestick upon it, an armchair, two other chairs, a wardrobe, and many books—all that was necessary, and nothing that was not.

Marcival came into his room and closed the door behind him. It was dark in the street, and the room was darker still. Marcival lighted the candle, and flung his cloak and his hat on to a chair. He walked to the cupboard, took out a half-full bottle, and bore it back into the candlelight.

Strange reflections of light, strange castings of shadow, seemed to make the pale face of the ascetic more haggard than ever.

Taking up a test-tube, he placed in it the fragment of gold which he had just bought in Lemberg's shop. On top of it he poured a small quantity of the liquid in the bottle. A dense vapour rose into the air and drifted away.

With the utmost exactitude Marcival analysed what was left at the bottom of his test-tube.

* * * *

A fortnight later the cavalier of the Arab steed emerged from Abraham Lemberg's shop. Albios swung himself into the saddle and was gone at a gallop.

A moment later the two myrmidons of Sartines were on his tracks. They disappeared round the corner of the street.

A street or two away, and Albios realised that he was being pursued. He spurred his horse. A moment later, and the mounted police galloped down the street.

A street or two away, and Albios appeared, riding at top speed. He looked behind him. A gateway loomed beside him. He swung his horse into its hiding.

The myrmidons dashed past the gateway, and disappeared into the distance.

Albios watched them go. He swung his horse around, and sped in the opposite direction like an arrow.

* * * *

In an obscure quarter, far from the centre of Paris, a house stood solitary.

In that solitary house, in his magnificently equipped laboratory, surrounded by his old books, his priceless manuscripts, his parcels of herbs, his mysterious vials, Cagliostro was working. Above him perched embalmed birds, casting over the comfortable surroundings of the chamber a sinister shadow.

A great furnace, with leaping flames, lit up his face, tense in its concentration. He was pounding in a mortar with a pestle; and, as he pounded, he enlightened the Count de Sablons on the purport of his experiment. All attention, consumed with curiosity, the Count watched the processes of the mage.

In the laboratory, and all around the house, brooded a deep silence.

The voice of Cagliostro echoed through that silence.

'Very soon, my dear de Sablons, you will be able to tell the sceptical that the Philosopher's Stone is no chimera, and that with your own eyes you have seen the making of gold. And perhaps, someday, you will be able to tell them that the Elixir of Life is no myth either.'

'How many years can the mages live who possess the secret?'

'Many years, my dear Count, very many years. So many centuries have I walked this earth that, despite all the events that I have foreseen, despite all the importance and the interest of my labours, I tell you that in truth I am getting bored.'

'Do you believe that it is possible to raise the dead?'

'Of course I believe it. Nothing is impossible. That, indeed, is the object of the work in which I am engaged, and I think that it will not be long before I find that which I seek.'

The Count de Sablons had come this day to the house of Cagliostro in search of the money that was needed to found the Egyptian Lodge, of which Cagliostro was to be the director and the guiding spirit.

To be initiated into the mysteries of Occult Wisdom was the dearest wish of the friends of the mage and of the Count de Sablons, and they looked forward with anxious longing to the day when the Lodge should be founded.

Cagliostro's work at the furnace was finished.

He handed some ingots to de Sablons, and walked over to an enormous chimney in the main wall of the laboratory.

He leant his weight upon a lever in the floor.

The metal screen of the chimney, about a metre and a half above the level of the floor, opened slowly.

Respectfully the Count de Sablons took his leave of Cagliostro, and, bending his body, he disappeared up the chimney.

Above the chimney, almost touching the ceiling, was a little bell affixed to the wall. At one side of the chimney, at the height of a man's head, was to be seen a small triangle cut in the wall, masked by a wooden eyelid.

Cagliostro leant his weight again upon the lever of the chimney. He went back to his work-table. Carefully he cleaned his instruments and laid them in their due positions.

Damping down the furnace, he cast a quick glance around him, and strode towards a piece of furniture, a kind of chest or closet, black as a coffin, which stood in a corner of the laboratory,

Only the last flickers of the dying furnace shed light upon the scene.

Cagliostro twisted a carving at one side of the chest. The lid of the chest swung open softly. From its interior a kind of platform, covered with a quilting of black velvet, rose up very gently. As the platform ascended there appeared the figure of Lorenza, clad in white, looking like a doll as she lay asleep.

With a tenderness too deep for words Cagliostro contemplated her.

Lorenza's enchanting smile was a magnet that might draw the stars out of their courses. The mage was swayed by the attraction of that adorable mouth. He approached her, and his lips parted as he bent to kiss her. Perhaps the lips of Lorenza were to triumph over the eyes of Cagliostro.

There they are, one against the other—the strength of the woman who smiles, and the strength of the man who glares. It is a spectacle worth watching.

Cagliostro was drawn and repelled. It was a great fight that was fought out within him. He could hold out no longer, he must yield, he must fall vanquished... No. The will of the mage asserted its dominion once more. He was himself again, strong and unscrupulous. He had all but touched Lorenza's lips when he checked himself, and the gesture of love was transformed into a gesture of power.

On the brow of this woman who lay there hypnotised, sunk in a deep sleep, he laid his hand, and his touch awakened her. She opened her eyes. Those beautiful eyes of the victim, charged with sadness and repugnance, gazed into the eyes of the poor mage. She made a movement as though she would flee from him.

'Lorenza, Lorenza my beloved, do I fill you with such dread? When you act so, you torture me beyond all your imagining.'

The voice of Cagliostro trembled for the first time.

Lorenza rose to her feet. She was no sooner afoot than she shrank away from him. Cagliostro went after her. Still she shrank away from him, away, away, with her eyes starting from their sockets, swollen with horror.

'I must away, I must away … I am afraid of you … Let me go, let me go! You are the Devil, and I shall be damned if I stay at your side.'

'You are mad, Lorenza. Whence come these fantasies of yours?'

'Give me back my liberty! Do you hold me as your prisoner?'

'You shall never leave my side. I have need of you beside me; and some day you will thank me for mastering you.'

'Yes, yes, I know it—I am no better than your prisoner; but do not forget that I know your secret…'

Feverishly Cagliostro sought to calm her, but she was not to be soothed. In vain he lavished all his tenderness upon her. Only when he made her fall under his hypnotic spell was he her master. He could do no other.

Fixing within her the talons of his eyes, the mage placed her once more within his power. He made her recoil toward the chest. There he laid her gently down upon the platform.

Suddenly he darted towards a small cupboard, opened it, and took out the document which the Count of Saint Germain had entrusted to him on that day of their 'memorable meeting in the cellars of the wine-press in ruins.

The face of the mage cleared as he found that the document was still in its proper place. He put it back, and closed the closet again. He raised his head, glanced towards Lorenza, and smiled. He approached her where she lay, almost transparent in her pallor. Ecstatically he

looked upon her as she lay sleeping, and his voice was bitter in its sadness.

'Why do you hate me? Why, why? If you but knew what it costs
me to fight down my passions of a man!'

He kissed her on the brow.

At this moment the bell upon the wall over the chimney rang
softly. At the sound of it Cagliostro pressed the lever of the chest, and
the platform bearing the form of Lorenza sank until it disappeared
within it. The lid closed, and Cagliostro advanced towards the
chimney.

Raising the little wooden eyelid which opened in the wall, he
looked through it into the next room. Then he leant his weight upon
the lever; and, when the metal screen of the chimney opened, he left
the laboratory by the same route as we saw the Count de Sablons
take a few moments ago.

*   *   *   *

On the other side of the wall, Cagliostro emerged into a corridor,
appearing through a chimney identically the same as the one we have
seen in his laboratory. He strode along the passage towards a door at
the other end. It opened, and a salon appears before our eyes.

Within the salon, Albios was desiring the Prince Rolland to be
seated until his master should be ready. As Cagliostro appeared upon
the threshold the servant withdrew.

Rolland rose to his feet and advanced towards the mage.

They exchanged a few words—we may suppose that they were
the time-honoured words of greeting which are customary on such
occasions—and then Cagliostro offered a chair to Rolland and drew
up another.

The Prince's conversation, of course, can register nothing more
than his passionate obsession. It can be concerned with nothing ex-
cept concentric circles around the Marquise de Montvert—a widow,
beautiful, rich, a person whose position at Court is an object of envy;
and, as though this were not enough, enamoured of Marcival, the

enigmatic Marcival. What more do you want to inflame any man's passion?

'Tomorrow night,' said Rolland, 'I shall be filling my salons with your best friends—all our old Strasbourg circle. So I shall provide you with the opportunity of keeping the promise you have made me in the matter of the Marquise.'

'I shall be glad to come. But, as for our friends of Strasbourg, I believe I have met almost all of them already at the house of the Count de Sablons.'

'Besides our old friends, perhaps I shall be able to present to you some important personages of Paris.'

Cagliostro bowed his grateful thanks. He would be present at the party without fail. With this promise Prince Rolland took his leave.

*　*　*　*

In the palace of Prince Rolland, in one of his magnificent salons, a great salon in the style of ... (in whatever style the reader pleases, so long as it is earlier than Louis the Sixteenth), Cagliostro sat enthroned within the circle of his worshippers.

Prince Rolland, the Count de Sablons, the Prince of Soubise, Jacques de Casanova, Professor Lavater and others less notable crowded around the chair of the mage, drinking in with breathless and respectful interest every drop of his marvellous and enthralling words.

(I beg my readers who do not know Don Juan, the real Don Juan, to follow with the closest attention the gestures and the attitudes of Casanova. He is a Don Juan in miniature, of words rather than of deeds, but, after all, that is better than nothing.

I would ask all students of physiognomy, too, to keep their eyes fixed on the head of Professor Lavater, the discoverer of the science of telling character by the bumps on the cranium.)

Cagliostro's words gratified his friends.

'It is agreed, then. On the night of the day after tomorrow the Egyptian Lodge will be founded, and then you shall be initiated into the first degrees of the Great Secret.'

'There will be some surprises for you,' said the Count de Sablons; 'persons of the utmost importance will seek initiation. There will be people of all political colours and all social classes.'

Others joined the circle, and it became even more animated as it swelled.

Suddenly Cagliostro fell still and made a strange gesture. He let his head droop backwards, and his eyes sank deep into the cavern of his skull. With a finger to his lips he asked for silence. His limbs became rigid, and he lay as if asleep in his chair. Only his lips murmured. 'Pardon me ... a moment. They are calling me.'

The mage turned into two. It was an amazing sight to see, but it was none the less real. A spiritual double, the image of his physical body, emerged from him, drew away from him, and vanished slowly into thin air.

The Prince's guests stood staring, unable to believe their eyes.

I take it that none of my readers will laugh at what I am presenting. This book, I hope, will fall into the hands of none who has not been initiated into the Hidden Wisdom.

* * * *

Far away from there ... the moon shone upon a road in Russia, a long, wide road hewn out of the side of a mountain, beneath whose height all the vast waste of the steppe lay shrouded.

Devouring distance, a sleigh drawn by runaway horses was swaying across the road, drawing ever nearer to a precipice that yawned wider at the speeding of the steeds.

Clinging to the reins with a strength redoubled by panic, the Grand Duke Anastasius and his daughter strove to bring the sleigh-horses under control, but in vain.

The sleigh raced towards the abyss, and the abyss raced towards the sleigh.

The Grand Duke's daughter—lest mortal men should be disillusioned—was beautiful to match her rank. Even the terror stamped upon her face could not mar the grace and harmony of her features.

Wearying of the sterile struggle against the mad onrush of the horses and the high tension of her nerves, the girl fell back huddled up into her seat, resigned to the catastrophe. Then, with her face illuminated by a light that shone from out of the depths of her memory, she groped feverishly in her bosom for a talisman, clasped it in her hands, and waved it in the air as though he called for aid.

Heedlessly the sleigh pursued its mad career towards the precipice. Realising his impotence, the Grand Duke let go the reins and abandoned himself to his fate. He drew his daughter into his arms in his anguish.

Despair was registered on both their faces.

All was over. There was no hope of escaping death. The precipice was but forty metres away. No, no, it was but twenty metres … Death, death … Death was smiling from the depths of the abyss.

But what was this? What had happened? The horses stopped suddenly. At the very verge of the precipice appeared the shade of Cagliostro, raising his two arms aloft. His body, his ethereal body grown enormous, barred the way before the maddened horses.

As if a nail had driven through it in its gallop, the sleigh halted a few yards from the edge of the abyss. The horses sniffed the air and blew great gusts of steam that clouded all the countryside.

Crossing himself, the Grand Duke was in the act of giving thanks to Heaven. His daughter seized him in her arms, kissed him passionately, and, opening her hand, showed him the talisman.

'Look, Father! The talisman that Cagliostro gave me has saved us. Do you remember what he told me? "If ever you are in danger, take this talisman in your hand and summon me".'

In the hand of the girl, under the rays of the moon, shone the talisman with the image of Cagliostro set in the middle of a triangle.

*   *   *   *

In the salon of Prince Rolland none dared to break in upon the dreaming of the mage. Around Cagliostro reigned a great silence. He lay there in the same hieratic attitude, rigid in his great armchair.

Then the fluid double of the mage returned and was restored to his body once more. Life flowed back into his face, and his limbs were full of its breath again. He opened his eyes. He looked steadily at the Count de Sablons.

'I have just saved the lives of your friend the Grand Duke Anastasius and his daughter,' he said.

With wondering eyes the bystanders gazed at the mage as if beseeching him to tell them what had passed.

Cagliostro recounted to his friends the adventure of the sleigh.

His tale was barely ended when the Marquise de Montvert, accompanied by a lady, appeared on the threshold.

Prince Rolland hastened to greet her.

One and all they rose to their feet at the coming of the Marquise, whose mien of a classical goddess drew all eyes and made all hearts beat faster.

Prince Rolland seized the occasion of the general stir to draw the Marquise aside, doing her the honours of his house and showing her the pictures and the treasures of art which he possessed. Step by step he led her towards the next salon. Deserted and dimly lighted, this salon seemed more suited for the talk of lovers.

Cagliostro followed them with his eyes. He read the thoughts of the Prince, and he smiled to himself.

Engrossed in all that Rolland showed her, the Marquise let herself be led away into the next salon.

It was a salon smaller than the first, but no less sumptuous. Imperceptibly the conversation drifted from the beauties of art which were the possession of the Prince to the beauties of person which were the possession of the Marquise.

To make use of a couch in the dim angle of a corner would be easy if the lady would but agree. There the couch stood ready, not quite in the corner but aslant, turning its back upon the darkest part of the room.

At this moment an Enchanted Prince, enchanted by the spells of his enchantress, the Prince could not let slip this unique chance of releasing the torrent of his thoughts in full flow. His words of love stumbled over one another, clove together, burned his lips. In their haste some words leapt in front of others, over those that should have had their turn before them. Others again reached the mark before their turn, and, surprised at their audacity, looked backwards and hung as if suspended in the air.

Patiently the Marquise heard them overflow their course, but none of them went further than her ears. She heard them until her nerves could endure their flow no longer.

'You know that another man has all my heart,' she broke in frankly.

The Prince reeled as though he would fall.

Then he pulled himself together and his words fell cruel in their deliberation.

'I know ... Marcival; but he will never love you.'

Eliane shrugged her shoulders. There was a lofty disdain in that shrug.

'I, on the other hand, shall love him always. He has revealed new things to me; he has opened to me the gates of the marvels of his soul, and since then I am not the same. Day by day the ways of the world matter less to me.'

Such words and such an attitude the Prince did not understand, could not understand, and did not want to understand. Instead of beating a retreat, he returned more insistently and more ardently to the charge. He seized her hands and kissed them passionately. Angrily she pulled them away from him, and bade him cease. She drew herself aloof, and begged him to let her be, to pester her no further, and to be good enough to leave her.

Standing before the great mirror in the salon, Eliane de Montvert set her ruffled hair and dress in order. As if in obedience to her request, Rolland returned to the next room where he had left his friends.

There, calling Cagliostro aside, the Prince told him of the rebuff that he had just received. Interrupting him in his telling; the mage strode towards the further salon. At the sight of him through the mirror in the distance, the Marquise turned round quickly with a welcoming smile on her lips.

Before Eliane had time to utter a word, Cagliostro advanced towards her. He raised his hand, in the gesture of one who sprinkles a liquid in the air. He hypnotised her, and he issued his command.

'Now, beautiful and most capricious divinity of the Court of France, I order you to love my friend Prince Rolland.'

Leaving her under the influence of his spell, Cagliostro withdrew towards the door, with his rigid hand still outstretched towards the Marquise. As he approached the threshold of the great salon his hand cut through the air in a quick movement, and he disappeared into the next room.

The Marquise awakened as the eddy of his movement reached her.

With his eyes Prince Rolland questioned Cagliostro as he came back towards the circle of his friends. An almost imperceptible sign from the mage sufficed. Rolland hastened to return to Eliane's side.

Seated on the couch in the dim corner, the Marquise received him with every mark of joy, and bade him sit down beside her. How changed she was from her earlier attitude! The artificial idyll began. As though he had forgotten the artifice that aided him, the Prince showed himself mad with delight. Perhaps he thought himself a real conqueror.

O love, in what corner of the world are you not to be found, and what weapons will your desire scruple to invoke?

Victim of the hypnotic command of Cagliostro, Eliane de Montvert felt all her antipathy for Rolland vanish.

Caught in the trembling hands of the Prince, her hands no longer sought to flee like startled birds. For the first time she smiled upon that love of Rolland which until now she had so rudely spurned. Burning with passion, Rolland grew bold, and his lips dared to approach the innocent face of Eliane.

At the moment when the two mouths were about to meet, behind them appeared Marcival. It may have been his body or his shade that stretched forth his hands above their two heads, and, with that one gesture, stayed the union of their lips.

Sombre and shadowy as those of a ghost were his words.

'Go your way freely, and let no strange force have power to change the rhythm of life.' Suddenly as he had come Marcival disappeared, vanished into thin air, dissolved into the shadows.

As though she awakened from a dream, as though she broke the chains of a spell, Eliane rose to her feet and passed her hands across her brow. At the sight of Rolland she could not restrain a shudder. She left him turned into a figure of stone.

When Cagliostro founded the famous 'Lodge of Isis', only a few privileged persons were initiated into the Great Secret.

In a narrow street of a low quarter was to be seen a crowd of people gathered around two rolling musicians who played the popular airs of the moment over and over again.

Someone had brought these two musicians here, someone had deliberately evoked this gathering of the populace. To what end? Perhaps so that no one should notice certain persons who made their way to a neighbouring house. Some of these persons are unknown. But I for my part have recognised the Prince de Soubise and the Count de Sablons.

They arrived one by one, mingled with the crowd which made a circle around the musicians, and then, with none remarking them, they glided away towards the low door of an old house of tumble-down appearance.

Slowly the strains of the music rubbed back and forth through the air their effacing rhythms.

*   *   *   *

In the cellar of the old house all was arranged in readiness for the foundation of the 'Lodge of Isis'.

Some fifteen persons were assembled there, seated in a semi-circle around a rough table. In the middle sat the Count de Sablons, reading the secret roll-call. His voice struck a note of solemnity as he ended his reading.

'Before we proceed to the final test, bear witness to these minutes, and swear to guard the secret and to obey higher orders.'

The minutes passed from hand to hand and came back to the president's place at the table whence they had started. The Count de Sablons raised his hand above them, and all the company rose to their feet and raised their hands too as they took oath.

Once the oath was taken the Count sat down again.

'The final test,' he said.

On the table at which the Count de Sablons presided stood a metal vessel containing dice-like objects bearing the names of all those present.

De Sablons shook the dice and made a sign. A blindfolded man was led up, put his hand in the vessel, and extracted a die, which he presented to the Count.

'Monsieur de Volney,' he read aloud.

From among the company Monsieur de Volney rose to his feet and stepped to the president's place at the table. The Count de Sablons took up two identical pistols, opened the breaches, and showed de Volney that one was loaded and the other uncharged.

Hiding the pistols under the table, he shuffled them from one hand to another and presented them to Monsieur de Volney, who chose one of them. Thus chance should decide the life or death of the new initiate, and the event should prove his courage and his submission in the presence of the utmost peril.

The Count de Sablons handed the pistol selected by Monsieur de Volney to the masked man, and led him to the wall at the end of the room.

Excitement and anxiety struggled for mastery on the faces of the company.

With his shoulders squared against the wall, Monsieur de Volney stood cool and collected. One by one those present rose and shook him by the hand. The Count de Sablons embraced him and withdrew.

Some ten paces away, the masked man awaited the order to fire. As the Count de Sablons raised his hand, he took aim and fired.

With his head held haughtily high, Monsieur de Volney looked on unmoved.

At the moment when the pistol was discharged the room was darkened and a great bowl of red wood, which had been half-hidden in the ceiling, began to descend slowly.

The bowl sank towards the place occupied by the Count de Sablons, who rose to his feet and went and sat among the company. When the bowl had reached the height of half a metre above the floor, the top part of it detached itself, and little by little rose back towards the ceiling, revealing Cagliostro within, in the attitude of a preacher in his pulpit.

Like the flash of a rapier Cagliostro's eyes of steel swept the assembly. With a curt gesture he bade them be seated. Then, drawing from his breast the document which the Count of Saint Germain had given him on that memorable night of the meeting in the cellars of the ruined wine-press, he unfolded it and began to read.

'Monsieur le Prince de Soubise.'

From his seat the Prince de Soubise raised his hand.

'Monsieur Jean-Jacques Rousseau.'

Slowly the famous philosopher raised his hand. Again the voice of Cagliostro thundered in that silence heavily charged with expectation.

'Monsieur Jean-Paul Marat.'

Swiftly, as though he had been awaiting the summons, Marat raised his hand aloft.

One by one Cagliostro called by name upon all those present until the list was ended. Then the Count de Sablons stepped towards him and presented to him the minutes to which the new initiates had sworn.

Cagliostro folded up the document and laid it aside for safe keeping. Then he addressed the company which hung upon his words.

'Now that you are worthy and that certain things may be revealed to you, you shall learn in what manner I was made initiate in Egypt more than three thousand years ago.'

The eyes of the assembly opened wide with curiosity, and the room narrowed in expectant waiting.

Like a patriarch who has seen all the centuries and all their happenings pass before his eyes, Cagliostro smiled slightly as he began his tale.

'When I had finished those profound studies under my master Althotas which had it as their object to lead me to the Supreme Knowledge, and after I had begged the Great Hierophant many times that he should deign to initiate me into the Mystery, there came a night when they made me swear that I should do my utmost worthily to pass the necessary tests, and then they led me from Memphis to the Pyramid of Cheops.

'Beneath a wan moon the waste of sand stretched towards the end of the world, such a great moon as that which we see in our evenings here, but a moon younger, finer and less weary than our moon of today. Like breasts rising and falling in anxiety the pyramids raised themselves into the night.

'The Pyramids! That concentration of the past in which are summed up all the centuries that are gone, in which those past centuries come back and live again, steeped in History, to impose themselves upon our eyes!

'The Pyramids! All those millenary mysteries, all that knowledge of the Pharaohs and the High Priests of that great people!'

With bandaged eyes Cagliostro walks slowly through our imagination between the Great Hierophant and his master Althotas. His steps leave deep tracks in the sands of Time, and upon the tight-stretched carpet of our watching eyes.

As the three of them drew nearer to the pyramid it grew higher and higher. It seemed to rear itself aloft, aloof and hostile, ready to defend its secrets. It was the Pyramid of Cheops, the greatest that mankind has ever yet learned to raise. All the universe bowed before it, was filled with the majesty of its mass, trembled beneath the weight of its magnificence.

The three men had reached the foot of the pyramid, and the Great Hierophant knocked upon one of the stones of its base. The block revolved and opened like a door, and the three men disappeared into Mystery. The block of stone swung and closed once more behind them.

'I heard it close behind me,' Cagliostro told all those who hung upon his words, 'as though Life itself had closed behind me and the world was cut off very far away from me. Encompassed within that silence of stone, we began to descend a long staircase. My eyes were still bandaged, and I was led by Althotas and the High Priest. At the foot of the stairway a great hall like a mortuary vault lay spread before us … We had advanced a few paces across the hall when the Great Hierophant removed the bandage from my eyes. He pointed to an enormous Sphinx at the end of the hall, and he spoke. "There is hidden the Book of Mystery, the Book of Life and of Death."

'We advanced to the foot of the Sphinx, and there the voice of the priest thundered again: "Follow your path where it leads, give proof of your strength of will, and never reveal the secrets. You will be numbered among the Lords of Time if you are victor over the five great tests."

'He placed the bandage over my eyes again and disappeared. Then my master Althotas took me by the hand, and together we plunged into the depths beneath the pedestal of the Sphinx.'

THE TEST BY EARTH

A stairway descended into the bowels of the Sphinx. At the end of the passage was a little iron door. Althotas and Cagliostro passed through the door and stopped on the landing beyond it.

Althotas led Cagliostro by the hand to the point where the stairway recommenced. There he unbound his eyes again.

'Go down this stairway,' he said, 'and count the steps as you go. At the bottom of them an abyss yawns before you. Draw back from it and retrace your steps if you are afraid.'

Slowly Cagliostro went down the steps that hung above the abyss. Althotas withdrew a few paces and stood watching in the shadow of the door.

Cagliostro kept on descending. Four steps were still below him before the stairway ended and emptiness began.

He went down two more steps, and then another…

At this critical moment Althotas opened the door above. 'Goodbye,' he called, and he disappeared through it.

On the last step of all Cagliostro hesitated a moment. His whole being shrank back from the abyss. Then he pulled himself together, poised his foot above it, took one pace forward, and fell...

'O my friends,' exclaimed the deep voice of Cagliostro, 'I tremble still at the thought of the horror of that moment. I fell down into the depths of the abyss, and I remember how all my body creaked as I moved, and how feverishly I felt my aching limbs, unable to believe that they were still in their proper place. I tore the bandage from my eyes, and looked about me on all sides to see what place was this into which I had come. At this moment a thick cloud of smoke arose before me, and in the midst of it appeared a horrible skeleton, a skeleton that moved and waved above my head an enormous scythe. Out of the skeleton or out of the walls there came a voice crying: "Malediction upon those who disturb the peace of the dead!"

'I could not make the smallest movement.

'Beneath the menace of the scythe I stood rigid. Then the skeleton raised an arm and pointed out to me a door that gave issue from those depths. He handed me a lighted torch. "Begone," he said, "begone from this emptiness narrow and dark as your mother's womb,"

'I seized the torch, opened the door, which clanged violently behind me when I had barely passed through it, and plunged into a passage as cramped as a pipeline bored through the bowels of the earth.

'How small I felt myself to be, how wretched and devoid of life as I dragged myself through that narrow tunnel like a worm, with no other light than that of the taper which I bore in my hand as though I carried my own star.

'I dragged myself along, I dragged myself along ... There was no air, I breathed with the utmost difficulty, I thought that I should swoon, and every other moment fatigue made me stop.

'I dragged myself along, I dragged myself along. The tunnel seemed interminable. My breast was oppressed with a load of anguish, a cold sweat broke out upon my forehead, my throat was parched, and every three paces the lack of air left me gasping all but insensible on the ground. I summoned up all my strength, and kept crawling along.

'I looked behind me, and the light of the taper showed me the way that I had come. I looked before me, and the light of the taper showed me the way that I had still to go. What despair was mine, what inexpressible anguish! There was no door, not even a crack to give me hope of the ending of this martyrdom.

'My eyes grew wide with dread. A mortal terror must have been painted upon my face. I could do no more. All hope deserted me. I fell for what seemed to be the last time and bowed my head to the ground in resignation.

'I am lost, I thought in my despair; I am doomed to die in this dreadful tomb.

'And then I thought: No. Where is my courage? Where is my strength? I have vowed not to fail, and I will not fail. Forward, forward!

'I know not whence I drew a last reserve of strength; but I went on my way, dragging myself despairingly along.

'Suddenly the taper revealed to me a bend in the tunnel. I turned it resolutely, found a further bend, and after three more turns found myself finally at an exit, more dead than alive.

'I left that horrible tunnel through a hole that was even narrower. But how can I tell you of my delight as I saw the light—a light which was not that of the sun, but that seemed to resemble it? I stood erect, drinking deeply into my lungs the pure air that fanned my fevered brow.

'Beyond the aperture through which I had emerged from the tunnel, another descending stairway offered itself before my feet. My knees were bending with weariness as I went down the steps. Two metres down this last stairway a door barred my path. I had no sooner descended the stairway and advanced towards this door than it opened of itself, as though inviting me to pass through.

'On the other side of it a spacious gallery appeared before my eyes. Two initiates approached me smiling. "You have accomplished the test by earth," one of them said. "Before you proceed you must swear that you will observe the most absolute secrecy concerning all that you have seen, and that never will you use your powers to serve your own ambitions or to disturb the rhythm of life."

'I raised my hand towards Heaven and swore, and then he who had taken my oath touched me on the shoulder, and with his finger pointed out to me the punishment...'

THE PUNISHMENT OF PERJURERS

'In a recess of the gallery I saw an enormous Sphinx whose eyes flamed and were darkened, and from whose nostrils streamed smoke. Her mouth opened, and a clamour of cries arose from within her body. A man writhed within the jaws of the Sphinx, which fell slowly, the upper upon the lower, into his burnt and broken flesh, crunching his body.

'As I glued my eyes to this horrible spectacle it seemed that a chill torrent rent my back in twain.

'Taking me by the hand, one of the initiates led me to a great door which opened groaning upon its hinges. He motioned to me to pass through and go my way. "Proceed," he said, "and do not retrace your steps; for to retreat is impossible."

'The door closed upon me and upon his words.'

THE TEST BY FIRE

'At the noise which the door made behind me as it closed,' Cagliostro continued, 'I looked back and saw that everything had disappeared behind that colossal wall of stone. I turned to continue on my way, but I had not yet advanced a step when a dense, choking smoke arose at my feet, and, in the opening and closing of an eye, an immense garden of flames bloomed as if by enchantment and closed in upon me on every side.

'A sudden terror seized hold upon me. As soon as I could master my nerves I flung myself into the midst of the wreaths of fire.

'Covering my face to save myself from burning and from blinding I ran through the flames. Like an arrow I sped through that immense bonfire until, without quite knowing how, without realising what I had done, I found myself on the other side of that garden of fire, which bloomed tirelessly behind my back.

'I was on the verge of a lake. Behind me was the fire, and before me was the water.'

THE TEST BY WATER

'If I was to go on my way there was nothing to be done but throw myself into the water. I did so without hesitation ... And then the lake, which had seemed still and smooth, turned suddenly into a roaring torrent which foamed over my breast.

'I fought against the current, but, for all my desperate efforts, it was all I could do to make headway even a little. The opposing current was transformed into a tempest, and the waves smote me on the head like angry fists. I strove against the fury of the waters. I sank, came to the surface, floated, and sank again.

'I thought that all was over, and that I was doomed to perish in that raging lake, when beyond a final wave the further shore appeared. The storm sank into calm.

'Upon the bank a cavern hewn out of the rock opened its jaws like a petrified dragon. As I emerged from the water I saw no other path before me by which to go on my way, and I penetrated into the cave.

'The cavern gave upon a gorge between subterranean walls of rock. Its exit was a little wooden bridge which linked two faces of **a** mountain.'

THE TEST BY AIR

'I dared that little wooden bridge beneath which lay the fathomless depths of the narrow, endless gorge.

'On the other side of the bridge a closed door offered to my feet a step raised from the level some two hands high. I climbed upon the step and beat upon the door. Nobody answered. The echo of my knocking resounded through eternity. The door remained shut.

'I knocked louder and louder than ever. Echo went on answering my blows from the depths of the ravine. The door did not open.

'Then, looking all about me, I saw above my head a thick metal ring carved in the fashion of the jaws of a lion. I seized it and pulled.

'At that very moment there happened something frightful. There was a deafening noise. The bridge and the platform on which I stood crashed to the bottom of the abyss, rebounding in their fall from rock to rock.

'I hung suspended in the air, clinging to the ring, gazing with terror-stricken eyes into the depths of the precipice above which I felt desperately for a foothold that was not there.

'Down in the profundity of the chasm, together with fragments of the bridge that had shattered into bits, I thought I could make out pieces of skeletons and human bones.

'Soon, I reflected, perhaps my own bones would gleam at the bottom of the precipice beside those of the foolhardy who, like myself, had dared the tests and had not been able to survive them to the end.

'It seemed to me that from deep within me a voice called me: "Poor ignorant and overbold man, the hour has struck when you must pay for your presumption."

'To look down into the depths of the abyss made my head swim. My arms were growing weary under the weight of my body, and I closed my eyes so that I should not feel the lure of the precipice.

'I was in the act of beating upon the door for the last time with my feet when it began to revolve slowly and bore my body round to the other side.'

THE TEST BY FLESH

'On the other side I found myself in a magnificent hall of an Egyptian palace.'

Broken with fatigue, Cagliostro appears before our eyes making his way towards a great chair of carved wood standing before a table.

He falls heavily into the chair. The table is set as though someone were expected, with wine jars and glasses, with the most varied dishes and the finest fruits.

Behind the chair in which Cagliostro is seated is spread a curtain as nobly wrought as the tapestries which one sees in dreams.

Thirstily Cagliostro seized a glass and drank its contents down, and as he drank it seemed that this man half dead with weariness came to life again.

With the second glass the past was erased entirely from his memory. He felt himself full of strength and vigour, as though none of those things which we have just witnessed had happened to him.

As though it fell from the sky, a strange music shed itself upon the room, enveloping the mage in the warmth of its melodious mantle. And at the sound of this music, which now seemed to burst forth from every object round about him, a group of unclad women advanced towards him, and began to dance around him in a dance such as no man ever yet has seen.

It was impossible to imagine faces and forms more beautiful. Not even the brushes of opium or of ether could paint such beauty.

Lustful in their mazes, the temptresses spread in a circle around Cagliostro. Desire such as he had never known before possessed his body.

A subtle fire coursed through his veins, as though the liquors he had drunk had turned into a fume of enchantment that sprang into life and movement every time one of these creatures of marvel approached him and offered him her charms, touching his hands and stroking his hair.

'This is the test by flesh,' thought the mage, 'the most to be feared of all the tests because it seems the least perilous of all, and because it comes at that very moment when reason is clouded by liquor and desire is cunningly aroused.'

Every time that Cagliostro felt his will failing him and bent his face forward towards one of these women, with his lips straining towards love, a priest hidden behind the curtain raised a dagger, ready to drive it into his back.

The women pressed around him and flung him flowers, and some even made so bold as to throw their arms around his neck.

Desperately, unable any longer to hold his instinctive impulses in check, Cagliostro rose to his feet and fled, flinging aside the bodies of the dancers who barred the way before him.

Covering his eyes so that he might no longer see them, he retreated step by step; and so he came into the temple of Isis, the great temple whose gateway opened at the end of the hall.

Followed by all his priests, the Hierophant advanced to meet Cagliostro where he stood, motionless in the midst of the temple spaces. 'Hail, O conqueror of the five great tests! Now you may learn the secret.'

Between the twofold file of priests the Great Hierophant and Cagliostro crossed the temple towards the statue of the Goddess Isis. Her veil was raised as they drew near.

The priests bowed down to the ground as the two entered the doorway in the pedestal and the veil fell again before it.

With searching eyes Cagliostro scrutinised the company that hung in reverent silence upon his story. A sentence more, and it was ended.

'So we both entered into that Mystery which may not be revealed.'

His eyes closed as though night had fallen suddenly, sealing the secrets of a cave of enchantment. The fingertips of the mage met together.

'If some day one of you should be worthy, he shall learn the Secret as his heritage. If not, the Secret dies with me.'

The upper part of the wooden bowl began to descend from the ceiling. It closed upon the lower, and the whole bowl rose again until once more it was half concealed among the rafters.

At the same moment a rain of flowers fell upon the company.

* * * *

With his head bent forward as though the weight of some anxiety pressed down upon his mind, Cagliostro made his way towards his house.

How many suns had risen and set within that brain of his! And who shall measure the matchless power of this man whose solitary steps resounded through the deserted streets?

As he turned a corner, deeply sunken in his own reflections, almost he brushed body to body against Marcival, who was coming from the opposite direction, almost with the air of a man who awaited him.

The two men saluted one another coldly. It seemed that Marcival was on the point of turning back, as though, perhaps, he had something to say to Cagliostro. He halted for a moment. But then he went his way, and, each following his own path, the two men were swallowed up in the darkness of the night.

*   *   *   *

In that room beyond the laboratory of Cagliostro, Lorenza was telling the story of her life to the Marquise de Montvert. Eliane listened to it with every mark of interest, and of the utmost sympathy.

'So you really live as a prisoner, and you may go nowhere outside your house?'

'As I have told you, Marquise, I am enclosed as within a prison, and sometimes there are whole weeks together when I may not leave this room. This is the first time since we arrived in Paris that I have been able to talk with anyone; and even now we are under the supervision of his creature Albios, who is like a faithful dog to him. You may be sure that at this very moment he is spying upon us, and perhaps trying to overhear our conversation. So you may understand that to me Cagliostro is no husband.'

'Then you do not love him?'

'Sometimes I believe that I loved him, above all before ... But now...'

'Now you no longer love him?'

'Now he fills me with fear, a dreadful fear. I want to flee away, I want nothing but to flee away from here, to leave his side as soon as may be. I believe that he has made a pact with the Powers of Evil. For pity's sake, Marquise, help me to escape from here! Surely you can find a way of saving me. I do not know why I place such confidence in you...'

'If there is anything that I can do, I will try to do it. But tell me, do you believe that what Cagliostro does is evil?'

'I do not know, I am ignorant of the ends that he pursues; but I would not be responsible for what may happen tomorrow. I want only to flee away, to return to my family in Italy, or to go and hide myself in a convent.'

'But do you suspect something?'

'No, I know nothing surely. I am afraid, and I know not of what I am afraid. This is no life; I had rather die than go on living thus, imprisoned as though I were guilty of some crime, though I have committed none.'

'Perhaps you are guilty of the crime of knowing too much about the doing of the mage?'

'Ah, my dear friend, if I could but ... If I could ... Silence, for pity's sake be silent!'

Suddenly Lorenza changed countenance.

'Here he is!' she exclaimed, full of dread. 'He is coming. I feel that he is coming, he is approaching the house ... Oh, my God, how long, how long! ... He is turning the corner of our street... He is coming ... I want to flee, let me be gone from here...'

'But my dear...'

'Silence, for the love of God ... He is at the door ... He is coming up the stairs ... He is here, he is here ... he is here.'

Cagliostro appeared at the threshold of the door, subdued and thoughtful. The fugitive smile that hovered on his lips was ready at any moment to flee away.

He advanced to greet the Marquise; but she shrank away from him in fear.

'You come from Hell, you come from Hell!'

Cagliostro's eyes of steel darted a question.

'What is this, Lorenza? What has befallen? May I assume that you have not abused the liberty which I have accorded you these past few days?'

'Liberty! Is this what you call liberty?'

'My love, what is amiss? You are pale, you are trembling.'

The eyes of Cagliostro, softened by tenderness, fixed themselves upon Lorenza.

'Let me out of this dungeon of yours!'

'Soon you may go free, soon, very soon; and you will be Queen among the Queens.'

'Soon? For three years past have I heard that word. I am wearied with promises; let me be gone from here. I do not love you. I have not been your wife, but your slave. I tell you that I loathe you.'

'Be silent, Lorenza, be silent!'

'Yes, I loathe you. You have made of me your instrument, you have held me because you had need of me; you have made me live the life of a martyr, and I can endure it no longer.'

'Be silent, Lorenza, be silent! Your words hurt me ... You cannot understand, but some day...'

'Yes, some day, some day! ... No, I will not be silent. I demand my liberty. I detest you, you fill me with...'

'Silence, I tell you!'

Cagliostro strode up to his wife, glued his eyes upon her, and laid his hand upon her head. She sank backwards suddenly.

'From this day forth you shall love me awake as you love me in your hypnotic dreams.'

As he spoke the mage lifted his wife in his arms, and carried her to a couch where he laid her softly down. He kissed her on the brow and issued his command.

'Awake, Lorenza; awake and obey!'

Lorenza opened her eyes, gazed at him lovingly as though he had returned from a long absence, flung her arms about his neck, and promised to remain with him always.

'Yes, my beloved,' said Lorenza—and how changed was her voice!—'I will follow you to the end of my life.'

Cagliostro smiled his satisfaction. He kissed her on the brow and strode towards the door. He disappeared through it with the air of a conqueror.

The door had barely closed behind him—his steps still echoed from the other side of it—when Marcival appeared beside Lorenza.

I know not whence he came, nor how he had entered. Slowly his shade drew near as though by successive stages it emerged from a mist; and as the mist gathered his body and his face assumed form and substance.

In his turn Marcival hypnotised Lorenza, and above the sleeping woman words fell from his lips.

'Go your way freely, and let no strange force have power to change the rhythm of life.' Noiselessly as he had come he vanished; and the sleeping woman did not even know that she had seen him.

While this scene was unfolding in the room beyond his laboratory, the mage in his great salon was making welcome two Ladies of Honour of Queen Marie Antoinette.

'Her Majesty the Queen has heard of the prodigies of Count Cagliostro,' said one of the ladies, 'and begs to invite him to her Court.'

'We are come in her name,' added the other, 'to ask you if you will come to Versailles tomorrow.'

'Her Majesty,' replied Cagliostro, 'has but to command and her commands are obeyed. I shall attend at Court tomorrow.'

'Until tomorrow, then, Count Cagliostro.'

'Until tomorrow.'

The two ladies rose to their feet, and Cagliostro escorted them to the door, where he bowed them farewell.

The Ladies of Honour of the Queen climbed into the coach which awaited them before the house of the mage.

* * * *

The coach was driving through the streets of Paris.

As it reached a crossing of two streets, one of the horses drawing the coach knocked down a wayfarer, a wayfarer who was one thought *too* thoughtful, a man of indeterminate age, that legendary age of men of tragedy. Immersed in his own reflections, the wayfarer was in the act of crossing from one footpath to another when the coach swung round the corner.

Beneath the horses' hoofs and the wheels the poor man fell to the ground.

The startled driver pulled up the coach.

People flocked around, and the Queen's two ladies descended from the coach to aid the injured man. He extricated himself even older again than he was when he fell.

He raised his hand to his head, and a stain of blood covered his fingers.

'He has cracked his skull,' cried one of the ladies pitifully; and she offered him a diminutive handkerchief trimmed with lace.

'It is but a trifle,' said the injured man; 'I am a doctor, and as soon as I reach my house I can staunch the blood within two minutes. It is a mere nothing.'

'But ride in our coach,' the lady insisted. 'We will leave you at your house.'

'Please tell us your name and address,' chimed in the other.

'Doctor Guillotin, 14 Rue de Saint-Louis.'

The doctor climbed into the coach, and it drove away from the midst of the crowd of gapers, that crowd of gapers which is the necessary chorus of any accident.

Gaily the coach drove away into the distance. O, innocent coach!

*   *   *   *

Cagliostro closed the door of his laboratory behind him. As he reached the middle of the room he looked anxiously on all sides, as though he sensed something untoward.

Stepping up to his table, he found a paper laid upon it at the place where he was in the habit of working. He picked it up and read it.

'Count Cagliostro, beware! Someone is dogging your steps. All that which is secret may cease to serve you. Already on two occasions you have dared to try and disturb the rhythm of life. Your punishment will be terrible, O great Copt!'

Without a moment's hesitation the mage strode into the next room. There he saw his wife sitting with her head between her hands. Without saying a word, holding his distance, he put her to sleep. With his arms outstretched towards her, he concentrated upon her all his hypnotic power. As a nervous tremor shook her and her head fell backwards he approached her.

'Lorenza,' said the mage, 'listen and obey!'

'What do you want of me? Order me, my friend,' breathed poor Lorenza through half-open lips.

'Bend your eyes upon my laboratory. Someone entered a moment ago and left this paper upon my table. Do you hear? Do you see?'

'Yes, I hear; yes, I see,' replied Lorenza.

'Who dared to do this? Tell me who was it that entered my workroom.'

Lorenza made no answer.

'Do you not hear that which I ask you?' Cagliostro asked anxiously.

'Yes, yes, I hear.'

'Then can you not see?'

'Yes, yes, I see.'

'Then why do you not answer me? Answer, I command you … Do you hear me? Obey me, and answer!'

'It is … it is…'

Lorenza's voice died away in her throat, and a frightful internal struggle was depicted on her face, as though a desperate battle, a battle to the death, was being fought out within the cells of her brain.

'What is the matter, what is wrong?' cried Cagliostro. 'Answer me, I command you, answer me!'

Lorenza's lips, shaken by a strange trembling, let no word escape them.

'I order you … my love, I beg you: answer me,' cried the voice of Cagliostro again. 'Do you not see who was there?'

'Yes, yes, I see.'

'Then why do you not tell me?'

A look of awful anguish was painted on Lorenza's face. Her lips barely moved.

'I may not tell you.'

Then a shudder ran through all her body, as though a kind of madness possessed her.

'Let us flee,' she cried, 'for the love of God, let us flee! Oh, I beg you on my knees, let us be gone! He who laid that paper on your table is stronger than you.'

With a gesture of rage Cagliostro flung himself out of the room, out of the house, out of the battle.

*   *   *   *

On the evening of the next day, in a salon at Versailles, courtiers and ladies of the Court, gathered around Louis XVI and Marie Antoinette, drank in the words of Cagliostro. He smiled a little as he observed the curiosity which his person excited.

The King had the face of a good man—a good man with a good man's face. There was something childlike in the expression and the manners of the Queen—the freshness of new milk bathed all her person, and she had something too of the innocent coquetry of early fruit.

But still it seemed that in the cheeks of the Sovereigns a flower drooped slowly into death. The lilies were dying.

All eyes were fixed upon Cagliostro, and all ears hung upon his lips.

The mage tendered to the Queen a bunch of flowers.

'I know that Your Majesty is a great lover of flowers; and since at this moment there are none in all Europe, it seemed to me that they would be a gift pleasing to your eyes.'

'More than pleasing, Count Cagliostro,' replied the Queen; 'pleasing and marvellous, since I know not whence you have been able to procure flowers at this season.'

'Flowers are living souls, Your Majesty. It suffices to give them a little of the warmth of the heart to enable them to live in all seasons. People may not know it, but so it is.'

'Then could you make me live those flowers that await the sun there in that flower-stand at the end of the room? I must warn you that only the stalks remain.'

'Every one of us has within himself something of the sun; but to release it and make use of it there is the problem.'

'Then you believe that it would be possible?'

'If Your Majesty commands...'

'I beg you, Count.'

Cagliostro strode towards the flower-stand, bent his body over it, then placed his hands upon it, raised them and held them a moment in the air. Then again he lowered them towards the earth of the flower-stand. Several times he repeated this gesture. Then suddenly he stepped to one side; and beneath his hands appeared the bare stalks putting forth flowers. The stalks rose and grew and the flowers opened before the eyes of his astonished audience as though the mage were some miraculous conjurer.

'It is marvellous, marvellous,' a hundred voices cried all together.

'They are right who claim that you work true miracles,' declared the King, who until this moment had been the most sceptical of all.

'It is miraculous, miraculous,' the Queen kept on repeating.

Cagliostro bowed before this cataract of praise, like an actor to the applause of his audience.

'Marvellous it is indeed,' said one of the ladies who had gone to invite him in the Queen's name as she approached the mage; 'but, with Her Majesty's permission, what we desire is that you should show us our future.'

'That I may not do,' replied Cagliostro; 'ask me what you will but this.'

'But this is the most interesting thing of all,' the Queen insisted.

'Your Majesty, I beg you that you do not ask me to show the future to any.'

'Perhaps the truth is that you cannot read it?' asked the Queen, as though to prick the *amour-propre* of the mage.

The question hit its mark. Its success was registered on the face of Cagliostro.

'I can do it, assuredly I can do it; but I should not do it.'

'But why should you not do it, Count?'

'Because ... because...'

'Because it is impossible,' added the Queen triumphantly.

'Nothing is impossible, Your Majesty,' answered Cagliostro, goaded by the pricks that the Queen inflicted on him; 'nothing is impossible, above all for certain men.'

'Then must we beg you, must we entreat you?' asked one of the Queen's ladies.

'I beseech you not to ask me!' cried Cagliostro.

'But I must tell you that my curiosity is even stronger than your request,' continued the Queen, visibly more interested than ever.

'Proceed, Count Cagliostro,' added the King; 'we will all keep the secret.'

The frown of Cagliostro revealed a certain perplexity struggling with a certain satisfaction in submitting himself to the test. Finally he made up his mind.

'So let it be. Since you insist so much...' He strode towards the great mirror at the end of the room, took from an inside pocket a little steel wand, and struck the centre of the mirror with it. Then he slid it towards one side of the mirror without taking it away from the surface.

On an instant there appeared in the mirror a regular cluster of severed heads, among which almost every one of the horrified spectators recognised his or her own.

The bleeding heads of the King and the Queen appeared in the first row.

A shudder ran through all the body of the Queen, but she strove to maintain her calm. 'But, Sir mage, what you show us there is the end of the world I' she exclaimed.

'No,' replied Cagliostro; 'it is not the end of the world, Your Majesty.'

'How horrible! How terrible!' breathed voices trembling with emotion. 'It is monstrous!' murmured others.

Cagliostro's reply was barely to be heard.

'I had warned you ... Never should one seek to see the future.'

'If it is not the end of the world, Count Cagliostro, it is at least the end of France,' spoke the calm and collected voice of the King.

'Nor is it that either,' answered the mage. 'Afterwards is to come the triumph of the Eagle.'

Again Cagliostro touched the mirror with his magic wand, and in a great picture appeared the figure of Napoleon, mounted on his white horse, dominating a field of battle like one who dominated History.

'And who is that?' asked the Queen.

'He is one who is making ready to be,' replied Cagliostro. His reply seemed to please him. 'He is one who lives already in your land, and whom perhaps Your Majesties have seen somewhere without taking notice of him.'

Here the vision changed, and from the depths of the mirror appeared an eagle. It approached, growing greater and greater. In the lower part of the mirror appeared a great globe, upon which the map of Europe stood out clearly. The shadow of the eagle swept across the globe, and waxed enormous until its wings completely covered it.

Suddenly, as though stricken by a shot, the eagle shuddered, hovered a moment, and began to fall headlong.

It fell, and fell, and fell...

The eagle fell and was dashed against the rocks of a distant island.

Hardly had the eagle touched the earth when on the same spot as if by enchantment appeared the figure of Napoleon, gazing sadly at the flowing and ebbing of the waves of the sea.

When that vision disappeared Cagliostro, too, had vanished, leaving within the walls of the Royal salon the stupor of mystery and the dread of prophecy.

* * * *

Cagliostro returned to his house. As he entered Lorenza's room he saw with angry surprise that his wife was not there.

Throughout the house he sought her, but all in vain. Lorenza was nowhere to be found.

He called for her at the top of his voice. Then he summoned his servant. Albios came running at his call. He had not seen her go out. He had fallen asleep for a moment. He knew not how, but it seemed that suddenly an invincible drowsiness had overcome him. Perhaps Lorenza had taken advantage of this moment to flee from her prison.

The mage clenched his fists.

'Someone has dared to cross my path!'

With his lips compressed in a line of anguish, with his face distorted with despair, Cagliostro seized his cloak and flung himself from the room.

Almost running he hastened through the streets, looking all about him. Suddenly he saw coming towards him on the footpath a girl of the city with a large basket on her arm.

He ran towards her, hypnotised her with no more ado, and bade her tell him where his wife was to be found.

Standing erect and rigid, with her face drawn backwards and her eyes fixed upon Eternity, the girl made answer through her clenched teeth. 'She has escaped from your house, taking with her certain secret documents which she is in the act of handing over to the police.'

The eyes of Cagliostro looked as though they would perforate the night. He closed his fists in a gesture of anger which emphasised the rage upon his face.

'Where is she at this moment?' he demanded eagerly.

'In an inn which is called "The Star of Gold," not far from Notre Dame.'

'What is she doing? What does she intend to do?'

'She has gone there on the recommendation of the police. Tomorrow she plans to flee far away from Paris.'

Cagliostro blew strongly upon the girl's forehead and awakened her. He dropped some pieces of money into her hand and strode away in agitation, followed by the stupefied eyes of the girl who, knowing nothing of what had passed, had for some moments been the instrument of his will. She stood there motionless between the street and Eternity.

Once more the mage returned to his house. Arrived in his laboratory he summoned Albios, gave him a dagger, laid his hands upon his servant's head and gazed fixedly into his eyes, making him the creature of his will.

'Go to the inn of "The Star of Gold" and kill Lorenza,' he commanded.

The body of the hypnotised man was shaken with a violent shudder as he heard the order. 'There is no other way,' added the voice of Cagliostro. 'Obey!'

Like an automaton Albios went out, walking straight in front of him with his eyes unseeing.

* * * *

It was a solemn night, a night which seemed to know its own importance in history.

(Reader, take any novel, and read in it the description of any night in which a grave happening is about to take place. Then resume this page.)

Albios reached the street wherein was to be found the inn of 'The Star of Gold.'

Opposite the inn, at the sight of his approach, a shadow glided a few paces away.

As if sucked into the maelstrom of Tragedy, Albios entered the inn.

The shadow turned back and passed again before the door of the inn. He let the mantle that covered his head fall back, and there was to be seen the narrow silhouette of the ascetic face of Marcival. That shadow was like a cross that sought to link Earth and Infinity.

* * * *

In a bedroom of the inn Lorenza lay sleeping peacefully as though nothing had happened, as though nothing menaced her, as though she knew that someone was protecting her while she dreamed.

Suddenly a trapdoor in the room, leading from the loft of the house, opened, and there appeared the face of Albios, with his eyes fixed.

Albios climbed through the opening and let himself into the room.

He strode towards the bed where Lorenza lay sleeping. He stopped beside her and raised his dagger above the breast of the slumbering woman.

In the street Marcival kept his gaze fixed upon another opening into the room, upon the window which gave upon the street, and which now presented a picture as of the background of the universe.

That window had now assumed a life of its own; it was filled with a soul of its own because of the momentary interest which it had assumed in history.

At the same moment when Albios was about to let his dagger fall and plunge it into the breast of Lorenza, Marcival in the street also raised his hand to Heaven, as though he sought to arrest Fate.

*   *   *   *

Albios stood with his dagger poised in the air, as though his arm were gripped in space by an invisible hand.

He made an effort to wrench it from that grip, but in vain.

He hesitated a moment, a shudder ran through him, then he turned on his heel and went out as he had come. His eyes were still fixed as he went his way.

*   *   *   *

Within Cagliostro's laboratory, Albios explained why he had been unable to fulfil his mission. He did not know what had happened. The avenging dagger seemed as though held in the air.

'An unknown force seized my arm and compelled me to leave the room.'

As he heard the words of his servant, in whose fidelity it was impossible for him to doubt, Cagliostro wrenched the dagger from his hand and hastened away to do justice himself.

* * * *

Watching over the dreams of Lorenza, Marcival stood sentinel at his same post in the street.

As he saw Cagliostro approaching in the distance, he crossed the street and vanished around the nearest corner.

Cagliostro had no sooner entered the inn than Marcival hurried back upon his tracks and raised his right hand towards the room where Lorenza lay.

* * * *

Upon the door-handle of the room where his wife slept Cagliostro laid his hand.

Finding that the door was locked and would not yield, he made his way along the corridor and into the loft, towards that trapdoor through which we saw his servant appear a few moments ago.

As though she had received a summons and an order Lorenza suddenly awakened, wrapped herself in her cloak, and hastened towards the door. She turned the key and left the room at the very moment when Cagliostro was entering it through the trapdoor.

Along the corridor Lorenza fled towards the staircase and hurriedly descended it. Behind her came Cagliostro in hot pursuit.

Every time that Cagliostro hastened his steps to overtake her, Marcival raised his hand and new speed was lent to Lorenza's feet also.

Lorenza reached the corner of the street, where, in a doorway, Marcival was lying in wait.

The three persons met, Lorenza more dead than alive, while Cagliostro and Marcival, face to face, glared into each other's eyes.

Marcival made a sign to Cagliostro, and the three made their way towards the house of the mage.

When they reached his house, Cagliostro motioned Marcival towards the door of the salon, and, taking Lorenza by the arm, led her to her room. Lorenza let him lead her without resistance.

The door which joined Lorenza's room to the laboratory of her husband stood open. Through this door Cagliostro went. As he passed through his laboratory he flung the dagger on the table. Then, through the shutter in the chimney, he made his way towards the salon where Marcival was awaiting him.

Sunk in a chair and in his thoughts, Marcival seemed to be far from the world, with his eyes, caught up into space like a diamond brooch, lost in the heavens.

Lorenza gazed into the laboratory of Cagliostro. Her eyes gleamed as she saw lying on the table the dagger which gave back the gleam in her eyes.

The light of a sudden decision shone in them. Crossing her room at a run, she entered the laboratory of the mage, seized the dagger, and with the strength of despair plunged it into her own heart.

* * * *

Ignorant of what was happening but a few paces away from them, Cagliostro and Marcival were tense in discussion.

Firmly but with no violence the voice of Marcival repeated:

'I demand that you leave Paris.'

'I am responsible for my acts to none.'

'Certainly you are responsible for your acts,' replied Marcival. 'The hour of your punishment has struck. Someone has dogged your steps, someone has kept a reckoning of your misdeeds, O misguided brother! He has observed that you have used the Secret and your power to disturb the laws of Nature and to serve your own ambitions. You shall be punished.'

Cagliostro smiled disdainfully.

'Who are you?' he asked. 'I do not know you, and I laugh at your predictions.'

Marcival looked at him sadly and unbuttoned his coat.

'Look, Giuseppe Balsamo!'

Cagliostro looked, and saw upon his breast a great white cross with a crown of roses in its centre.

'The Grand Rosy Cross!'

Silently, profoundly sorrowful, Marcival made his way to the door and left the room and the house.

* * * *

Returning to his rooms, Cagliostro entered Lorenza's chamber and found himself confronted with a horrible sight.

The body of his wife lay dead upon the floor in a pool of blood.

The mage stood as though turned into stone. Anguish, despair, and anger strove for mastery upon his features.

He knelt down and embraced the body, caressing her brow with a tenderness foreign to his character. Then roughly he let the body fall, and burst into a bitter cry of rage and grief.

'O unhappy creature, why did you not understand me, why did you not love me? With your love I would have changed the face of the world.'

Now, in the presence of the corpse of his wife, the mage felt awaken within him all his passion as a man. Now that it was too late to go back, he felt an infinite tenderness that overflowed his heart. He understood how wrong he had been ever to master his heart of a man, and coldly use as a mere instrument the women whom he loved. For now he knew that he had really loved her.

Now he understood. Now he saw clearly. He had prepared everything for his triumph. Like a general on the field of battle he had sought to forget no detail. And he had forgotten love.

He had forgotten love, the sole indispensable thing, the only invincible power, the only lever which can move worlds.

* * * *

It was in the salon of the Marquise Eliane de Montvert.

(It was a salon more or less the same as any other of the period—that is to say, a salon in somewhat better taste than the majority of the salons of today, with furniture which would be the delight and make the fortune of more than one antiquary.)

Marcival and Eliane seemed to be far from the world, outside the limits of our atmosphere among who knows what stars unknown to us, wafted away by the charm of an intimate conversation, full of the warmth of those two privileged souls born to understand each other. 'I understand perfectly all that you have told me,' said the young Marquise, 'for I have grown accustomed to your way of life and thought, and my sole desire is to be your fellow-worker, your comrade in the task which you have undertaken.'

'I have as much confidence in you as in myself,' answered Marcival; 'for the eyes of your spirit have been opened to the sun like a flower of the dawn, and when the eyes of the spirit are truly opened they never close again.'

Eliane seized the hands of her friend and kissed them tenderly.

'Therefore,' he said, 'our souls are united like a shadow to a man, for life and for eternity united, my friend, for the achievement of our great task. The struggle will be relentless. Black Magic is very strong, and, since it shrinks from nothing, it has more weapons than White Magic.'

'That does not matter. We shall work until we have cleansed the world of all these men of learning gone astray, and of all deceptive sects and cults. O my friend, how glad I am to think that I can be of service to you and that I can be your helper, the comrade of the confidences of your soul.'

Their hands joined and clasped as though to seal an oath to the world.

*   *   *   *

Upon a table ordered by way of a catafalque, covered with black velvet, lay the body of Lorenza between four lighted candles. How sad it was to see that beautiful body, but a few hours ago so full of life, now so full of death!

Seated in a chair in a corner of the room, with his head in his hands, Cagliostro kept vigil beside the body of his wife.

The mage seemed sunk in a dream of sorrow, as if overwhelmed by his grief—that grief that revolved like a hundred windmills in his brain and his breast and his veins.

The bell high up on the wall of the laboratory over the chimney rang softly. Immersed in his meditation Cagliostro did not seem to hear it.

The bell rang again, repeatedly and more loudly.

As though he awakened the mage raised his head, stood up, and, slowly and heavily, made his way out of Lorenza's chamber into the adjoining laboratory.

There, having reached the chimney, he looked through the little triangle cut in the wall.

With a pressure of his foot he worked the lever, and the screen of the chimney was raised, to give admittance to Albios.

'Three unknown persons are awaiting you in the salon,' he said.

Cagliostro prepared to meet them.

'Albios,' he murmured, 'make ready for a long journey. We shall start this very day.'

* * * *

The three mysterious persons were seated in a semi-circle in Cagliostro's salon, with the air of judges.

When the mage appeared, he who was seated in the centre pointed to a chair drawn up before them and motioned to him to take his seat there, as though he were a man accused.

He handed him a document, and his words fell sternly.

'You know well, Count Cagliostro, that we who are here present are three Masters. Read the sentence of your punishment. You will see that you stand accused of prevarication and of working in pursuit of your own ambitions. You are accused of failing, through the love of a woman, to guard the secrets, and of allowing an important document to fall into the hands of the authorities. Five of our brethren have been arrested and thrown into the Bastille.'

'I swear to you that this is not my fault,' Cagliostro interrupted.

The other continued.

'I suppose you have not forgotten your meeting with those of the Rosy Cross, in the vaults of our old wine-press in a corner of Alsace. I suppose that you have not forgotten your oath, or the words of warning with which your labours were entrusted to you. Your fault is too grave, and your punishment shall be proportionate to it.'

Cagliostro listened to his words with an air of resignation.

'You shall be punished,' the mysterious person added, 'and your wife also shall be punished inexorably.'

At these words Cagliostro rose to his feet, 'One moment,' he said.

He left the salon, went to Lorenza's chamber, took up her corpse in his arms, and returned to the salon bearing that beloved body, a light burden for his Herculean strength.

As they saw him enter the three persons rose to their feet in their turn.

Cagliostro's words were barely to be heard. 'You have come too late. The sentence is already executed.'

The body of Lorenza sank from his arms to the carpet. Cagliostro raised his head, and in his eyes shone once more his former pride, his will of iron, and a new hope born of a sudden idea.

Calm and stern as ever, the three persons left the room.

*   *   *   *

In his laboratory Cagliostro piled upon the floor his secret papers, his rare books, his marvellous manuscripts.

Opening a cupboard he took out a vial and poured its contents on the documents. A flame leapt up consuming all his treasures—consuming, too, the last trace of anguish that lingered in his eyes, as though it would wipe out a whole tempestuous past.

'Nobody shall ever know what I have known,' exclaimed the mage.

Then he summoned Albios.

'Give me the Elixir of Life and the preparation which I have just compounded to call the dead to life again.'

'Sir, do you think it possible?' … 'All things are possible.'

Albios went to the cupboard and took out two vials, upon one of which was to be read, 'Elixir of Life', and upon the other 'Vita Mortis'.

Cagliostro took the two vials from the hands of Albios and placed them beneath his cloak.

'Far away, very far away, we shall begin a new life.'

'Heaven grant that it may be possible,' Albios responded.

The flames leapt up again, casting their light upon those faces stamped with suffering and tragedy.

* * * *

Before the door of the house the mage's coach stood waiting—that same black coach, almost funereal in its aspect, which we saw appearing out of the midst of a tempest in the first chapter of this tale.

Albios arranged the baggage and exchanged some words with the coachman, some words indispensable to fill Time and Space: the space that separated them from one another and the time that divided them from the coming of Cagliostro.

Cagliostro appeared on the threshold of the door, bearing in his arms the body of Lorenza.

He came down the steps and mounted the coach. Albios leapt in behind him, and the coach, drawn by its historic horses, started off at a trot.

Behind, the house was burning. Great flames devoured it, and a black smoke went up to the sky.

Ahead, a long road extended towards the horizon.

The coach reached the end of the way. In the distance the little rear-light winked its almond-shaped eye.

A cloud sank slowly to the ground, and within this mysterious cloud the great mage was lost to the eyes of the world.

* * * *

And afterwards? Whither did he go to seek refuge? Was he able to conquer Death? Does he still live somewhere with his beloved?…

THE END

AFTERWORD
to the Second Edition

In the 1920s, Vicente Huidobro busied himself with a number of artistic projects, *apparently* moving on from his earlier avant-garde poetry, which had made his literary name in 1917-18. 1921 saw the publication of a French-language selected poems, *Saisons choisies*, and then in 1925 Huidobro published two further poetry collections, both also written in French, which represent a transitional phase in his verse. However, he was also at this point in the midst of writing the great long poem, *Altazor*, and published the first sections from that work in Spanish-language journals in 1925. In 1928 be began writing the long prose poem, *Temblor de cielo* (Skyquake), and also the novel *Mío Cid Campeador* (published in this series as *El Cid*).

In 1923 he had published an anti-British diatribe, *Finis Britanniae*, and claimed that he had been attacked by British agents in the wake of its publication. This was a recurring trope in the author's life: it was to happen again with some Italian agents after he published an anti-fascist poem called 'Fuera de aquí' (Get out of here), and he was attacked twice in Santiago while running for President. Without wishing to cast doubt on Huidobro's honesty, it has to be admitted that he was very adept at getting publicity for himself and for his various projects, and I suspect that one or two of these incidents, at the very least, were less than they were made out to be. All gained him headlines. The decade also saw the publication of the author's collected manifestos (*Manifestes*, 1925), and a collection of essays and aphorisms, *Vientos contrarios* (Contrary Winds, 1926).

Huidobro had been fascinated by the new medium of film for some time and was reported by the *Paris-Journal* of April 1923 to be at work on a 'Cubist' film, which would revolutionise viewing habits. A month later, another newspaper *L'Ère nouvelle*, in an article on 'Poets and Cinema' reported that Huidobro had 'completed the scenario of a film *Cagliostro*, in which the specifically cinegraphic action is 'visualised' with an acute sense of optic rhythm.'[1]

---

[1] I am indebted here to René de Costa, who reports this in *Vicente Huidobro: The Careers of a Poet* (Oxford: Oxford University Press, 1984).

Huidobro reported that the film had been shot in late 1923 by the Romanian director Mime Mizu, but that it had been scrapped due to dissatisfaction over the editing. No trace of the film survives, although there are three pages from a script, written in French, in the author's papers, as well as a letter signed by Mizu confirming the veracity of Huidobro's statement concerning the film. There is a curious parallel here with the formal documentary evidence concerning a disputed publication of the poetry collection, *El espejo de agua* (The Water Mirror, 1914; 2nd edition, 1916), and one wonders whether the author might have been concerned over the possibility of a renewed accusation of dishonesty, of the kind he had suffered in 1918.

A revised version of the script was submitted to The League for Better Motion Pictures in New York and won a $10,000 award on 20 July 1927 as the best candidate for conversion into a film. On 23 July 1927, the *New York Times* reported, under the headline 'Chilean Gets Film Prize':

> Vicente Huidobro, young Chilean poet and novelist, was announced yesterday as the winner of a $10,000 prize offered by the League for Better Motion Pictures for the book of the year having the best possibilities for moving-picture adaptation. The book, still in script form in the hands of Paris publishers, is called *Cagliostro* and is based upon the life of the eighteenth-century necromancer and popular mystic.[2]

Alas for the author, this was just at the point when the 'talkies' arrived— *The Jazz Singer* was released on 6 October, 1927—and this style of silent film-making was rendered immediately outmoded.[3] However

---

[2] It should be noted that, notwithstanding reference to a 'script' in the newspaper article, the award certificate refers to a 'novel', and that a further newspaper article on 24 July, documenting the award ceremony, likewise refers to a novel. As far as I am aware, the typescript submitted to the Prize has not survived.

[3] *The Jazz Singer* was not in fact the first sound film. It was however the first full-length feature film with synchronized singing sequences and [some] synchronized speech *as well as* synchronized instrumental score and sound effects. Previous films, notably *Don Juan* (1926) had already offered synchronized score and effects, but no previous full feature had had all that

the novella, which has many cinematic elements, was published in English translation in 1931 in both London and New York, to positive reviews. It appeared in the original Spanish only in 1934, in Santiago, Chile, where it made no impact at all. The present edition reproduces the text of Wells's 1931 translation, with only some minor edits to the text, where today's usage has diverged markedly from that of the 1930s, or where the original appeared too awkward for modern tastes. It should be added here that the Spanish-language edition had a shorter Preface than the one translated by Wells, but we have not altered the Preface here to take account of that. That edition also had a brief 'To the Reader' and 'Introduction' following the Preface, which I have translated and added to this edition, partly for the sake of completeness, but also because they amplify the cinematic elements of the whole volume.

While Huidobro's career in the film world had come to a sudden end, the extra cash was no doubt welcome, and he managed to make the best of it, rapidly gaining publication for the novella in English, as well as for the *Cid* novel—the only English-language book publications of Huidobro's work during his lifetime. As a souvenir of his days in the film world, Huidobro also had a number of photos of the stars—including Gloria Swanson and Greta Garbo—and a peculiar group photo with a number of starlets (see p.6 of this volume): Lya de Putti (1897-1931, Hungarian silent-film actress); Norma Smallwood (1909-1966, Miss America 1926), Roberte Cusey (1907-?, Miss France 1926, who made two films in 1927-28), a certain ballerina by name of 'Miss Tomiris'⁴ and Jacqueline Logan (1904-1983), known as the 'Venus of New York', but also one of the stars of *King of Kings* (1927), where she played the role of Mary Magdelene.

Tony Frazer

The Jazz Singer offered, and the world of the movies changed overnight. Sound-on-film recording technology (as opposed to sound-on-disc, used in *The Jazz Singer*) was to be the key to the Talkies' complete success, and this technology was being used from 1930 onwards.
⁴ This *may* refer to Helen Tamiris (1905-1966), dancer and choreographer, who was active at this time.

CPSIA information can be obtained
at www.ICGtesting.com
Printed in the USA
BVHW072041101120
593011BV00002B/166

9 781848 616585